THE Billionaire's BILLBOARD PROPOSAL

ROSE M. COOPER

OSHUN
PUBLICATIONS
oshunpublications.com

The Billionaire's Billboard Proposal by Rose M. Cooper
Published by Oshun Publications
9 Old Kings Road STE. 123 #1038
Palm Coast, FL 32137
www.oshunpublications.com

Book design by Oliviaprodesign
www.fiverr.com/oliviaprodesign
ISBN: 978-1-950378-91-3 (Paperback)
ISBN: 978-1-956319-36-1 (Hardback)
ISBN: 978-1-950378-90-6 (eBook)

GET YOUR GENRE FIX
TODAY! JOIN MY
NEWSLETTER FOR MY
RECOMMENDATIONS AND
UPDATES!

ROSEMAECOOPER.COM

THERE ARE ALSO AUDIOBOOKS!

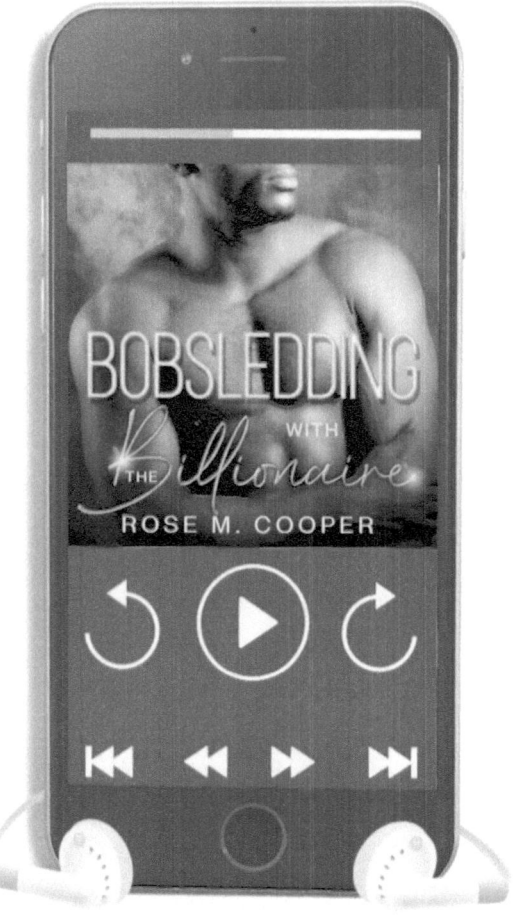

Camryn Javion Alvarez

THE SMELL OF BURNED BACON FILLED THE KITCHEN even after Stella had been soaking the pan for at least half an hour. The open French doors welcomed a breeze so lazy that it barely moved the white, filmy smoke wafting through to the living room.

This area of the house was open-plan, so she could see the man from the TV satisfyingly clearly. She let herself look at the man for only a moment before she organized her thoughts and snapped her gaping mouth closed. She wouldn't get many of these dishes finished if she continued to gawk at him.

She hadn't been the one to burn the bacon. A few years of cooking non-stop for a household made it next to impossible to burn things, she'd learned. If she let her mind wander, she could remember a time when cooking wasn't a chore and kitchens were filled with warmth and laughter. She snuck a glance at her aunt, who was counting her vitamins on the quartz counter. Eleanor had done enough for her to make questioning her generosity unthinkable. Nonetheless, sometimes she couldn't help but wonder if the only family she had

1

left loved her. She sometimes felt as though they didn't even like her.

No matter. She shook her head, hoping her unhelpful thoughts would clear faster than the still-present blanket of smoke in the kitchen. Stella dipped her hands into lukewarm water and gave the black-faced pan a violent scrub. The char on it didn't budge. She sighed, wrinkling her nose against the smoky smell. Every now and then, her aunt would get the inexplicable desire to help with making breakfast. This had, without fail, always resulted in something getting burned.

When the familiar tune blared from the TV, she didn't stop herself from turning to the TV, craning around Eleanor's body for a clearer view. She knew him, from his middle name to his favorite color. Camryn Javion Alvarez's gray eyes pierced through her aunt's flat-screen TV. Her gaze flitted away, back to her pot, cheeks burning, as she wiped her hand on her apron and swallowed the last bite of her toast with a wince. She probably should have chewed on it more.

She was being silly; she knew. She'd never even met him.

"I'm running so late," Stella muttered under her breath.

Her aunt barely spared her a glance. Her mouth was moving, still counting her vitamins. Her cousins began a new round of fawning over one of the magazines strewn haphazardly on the couch. Mackenna was leaning against the loveseat, her body angled toward the French doors. "I wonder when he's going to start dating again," she said, her thumb flicking quickly over her phone. "It's been like a year."

"Eleven months," Julia specified. She sighed dreamily, looking up at the ceiling as though she could see something they couldn't. "Just a few more days, and I'm certain he'll have a new and improved girlfriend." She gave Julia a knowing look as she spoke, and the two burst into a fit of giggles. Mackenna, who was about Stella's age, rolled her eyes at her little sisters, but Stella noted the smile she bit back. Whenever Julia and

Kiana talked about Camryn Alvarez, it was as if they were suddenly teenagers again, not acting at all like the twenty-four-year-olds they were.

The debut of her aunt's latest fashion collection was just two weeks away. Eleanor had been buying animal print wallpaper and renting elaborate artwork of lions and zebras, piling them in the garage in preparation for the intimate celebration they were going to host on the day of the collection's launch. Stella knew her family well enough to infer that "intimate" probably meant more than fifty people.

Camryn Alvarez, hands down the wealthiest businessman in Naples—and most of America—would be there, at least according to Eleanor. He was known to support local businesses. It was only logical. Rubbing shoulders with the social elite of Florida would give him a good name, and a good name meant America would love him. America loving him would get him more customers for the family business he'd been running for almost five years; it was a well-acclaimed consulting firm. Of course, getting more customers would mean he would make more money.

And rub shoulders he did. Stella could barely comprehend that she might see him face-to-face in just a few days—if her aunt let her go.

Camryn had been a national celebrity for years. Featuring in magazines like Seventeen when he was in his early twenties and then maturing into Cosmopolitan and even Time Magazine after turning thirty. None of this had really impressed Stella, though. It was only after he started giving back to the community that she'd been drawn to him.

Seeing a picture of him with newly born puppies snapped at a local animal shelter had sealed the deal. Ever since that day, she'd resigned herself to begrudgingly fangirling over him. No sane woman she knew could resist a handsome man with puppies in his arms, and it wasn't as if she was the only woman in America who found him attractive.

As if to prove her point, Julia and Kiana squealed again, gaping at the TV. It was another Alvarez Consultants ad. Camryn strode purposefully in slow motion across a road leading to a towering building that boasted Alvarez Family Consultants in a bold, golden typeface on the screen. The building had a black, almost matte façade, and its single spire waved an American flag that stood out brilliantly against the black. Stella's heart fluttered as the camera zoomed in slowly to capture the dark hair at the nape of his neck in perfect clarity. "Alvarez Family Consultants. How can we help you?" The voiceover and crescendo of the background music were brought to an end by the beginning of a telenovela.

She turned her soapy hands back to the kitchen sink, frowning down at the stubborn pan.

"Stella, dear?" She turned to find her aunt watching her with her lips pursed. A sense of foreboding crept up her spine. What had she done now? "You know we truly appreciate you, dear, but really, could you refrain from serving us raw eggs? We would appreciate you even more if you did." Eleanor gave her a small smile that made her feel about as small as an ant, even though she towered way over her aunt.

"I second that," said Mackenna, who was now seated on the bright pink loveseat.

Stella bit the inside of her cheek. At the corner of her eye, their four plates winked brightly at her. She had just washed them, so she knew for sure that each one of them had eaten all the food on their plates, including the eggs. Julia was staring at her with mocking eyes as she leaned over the couch she was sharing with Kiana, as if Stella's torture was more fascinating than the show playing on the TV.

Stella sighed. "I'm sorry, Eleanor. I'll do better next time." She'd been saying the same words since she moved in with her aunt four years ago. It occasionally made her feel like a child. No twenty-eight-year-old woman should have to apologize as much as she did. But what could she do? If it wasn't for her aunt's generosity, Stella would have been out on the streets. She couldn't—wouldn't—let herself forget that she was indebted to these people.

Anyway, Eleanor's words didn't really surprise her. Every now and then, they would claim that the meat was suddenly not as rare or as well done as they liked it, or that the smoothies she made were "over blended". She couldn't judge her aunt too harshly, though. Between tying loose ends for her party and making sure all the models she hired still fit perfectly into their outfits, Stella would have gotten a little cranky herself in the same situation.

She glanced down at her phone as she turned back to the sink, gasping when she saw the time. "I'm late!"

None of her family said anything, but it didn't bother her. She'd gotten used to only being spoken to when she was needed.

Bolting for the front door, she jerked back to the kitchen to neatly fold her apron into the cupboard beneath the sink. Her dark messenger bag was waiting for her on the sleek credenza table in the entryway. She slowed to close the door gently, knowing that her aunt would have a word or two for her if she slammed it, even if she was late.

Working for Uber Eats had its perks. Well, just two, really: the pay and the views she got to have whenever she delivered out-of-town orders. The wind cooled her neck as she cruised down the road on her old scooter, hedged in by wheat fields on one side and wild grass on the other, the sun glaring down on her mercilessly.

She slowed down and negotiated a curve, then stopped before a bronze, ornate gateway while the engine was still grumbling obstinately. The scooter had been given to her by her dad as her twenty-second birthday present. Something twisted in her chest, as it always did whenever she thought of her parents. She was forgetting their faces more and more as the years blurred past. They'd been very old-fashioned ("photos are for people who live in the past"). Consequently, she only had two pictures of each of them. One of them together as a family; she was standing between her mom and her dad, smiling with a missing tooth.

A camera stuck onto the brick-faced wall that held the gates in place jerked to face her. She waved awkwardly. A loud buzz pierced through the peaceful scene, and the gates swung open. She felt silly on her fading sky-blue scooter as she neared the modern palace. The brown-gray cobblestone pavement, unmarred by weeds, led to a large, slightly aristocratic manor with a roof that swanked triplet empyrean steeples. The mansion peered haughtily down at her as if to say, "Are you lost?"

Stella bit her lip as she pulled the key out of the ignition and set her helmet on the seat of the scooter. Gathering the order—two boxes of pizza—she walked up one of the two curved stairways that flanked a Grecian statue of the upper body of a man. She took a deep breath, squared her shoulders, and then tapped the brass knocker firmly against the large door.

A breeze ruffled her hair into her face, and she flicked it back. She had always found driving out of town in her little bipedal scooter a little intimidating outside of the city, with only open-air fields and a few manor houses for as far as the eye could see. Still, it was also quiet and peaceful out here.

She heard the muted tap of footsteps from behind the door and smiled brightly to greet her customer.

The door gave way with a slight groan. A cold thrill went up her spine at seeing the man on the other side of the doorway. A moment later, as if it had needed time to register what her eyes had already taken note of, her heart began to thunder beneath her rib cage like a wild thing.

Dark hair. Gray eyes. Camryn Javion Alvarez stood before her.

The Delivery Girl

CAMRYN SET HIS GLASS OF SPARKLING CHAMPAGNE on the tray of a passing waiter as he made his way to the dance floor. He was heeding his father's insistence that he dance at least once this evening.

He had been inebriated only once in his entire life, and not on purpose. His sister Amelia had yet to cease making fun of him for being such a lightweight, even though more than a decade had passed since his eighteenth birthday party. He would never forget the hangover he'd gotten the day after; it was as though his brain had been trying to squeeze out a replica of itself. Now, he only ever drank at work functions, like the one he was at tonight. Even then, he let himself have only one drink—two if he was feeling adventurous.

He felt his father's heavy gaze like a laser between his shoulder blades as he lingered on the edge of the cluster of dancing bodies, leaning on one of the chairs surrounding the mostly empty round table adorned with abandoned glasses of wine and champagne. Sebastian Alvarez had strange notions about what it took to please the media. Just a few years ago, he had dictated—or tried to dictate—everything Camryn did, from where he was seen to who he was caught with, before he one day stopped abruptly. He went heavy on the small details now, like whether or not Camryn danced at work parties or was exercising regularly, as if Camryn didn't have a paid personal trainer bearing down on him enough on the latter.

That watchful gaze had driven him crazy when he was younger. These days, as his father's hair grayed more and more, Camryn found that he didn't mind it much anymore. The tyrant who really drove him crazy was his mother—his beautiful, wise mother. Ever since he broke things off with Clare, she'd been hounding him about getting her grandbabies to worry over. He couldn't find it in him to tell her the real reason he and Clare weren't together anymore. Heck, he could barely even tolerate thinking about it himself. If he could get away with it, he would never talk about her again.

But how would he get himself to stop thinking about her? The memories of her pounced on him when he least expected them.

He released a slow breath and rolled his shoulders, turning his head to look at the stage. The voluptuous woman holding the microphone flicked her wrist almost imperceptibly. A moment later, the fast-paced, jazzy number slowed to a soulful melody. He couldn't help the slight smile that took over his face when she lifted the microphone to her mouth and sang in a voice that washed over him like velvet. On the dance floor, couples wrapped their arms around each other.

He and his sister were the driving forces behind bringing the family firm into the twenty-first century. Modernizing everything from the entertainment they hired for work functions to the diversity of their employees. He had never thought of his dad as racist. Still, about seven years ago, when an African American reporter had asked him during a press conference why so few of the workers in the company were non-White, it had shaken him. It wasn't done deliberately by the company, of course, but she had been right. They were a consulting firm, and if they could diversify, it would really boost business and help disadvantaged classes.

For the first time, he felt a passion for the family business replace the begrudging duty that had always driven him before. With Amelia's enthusiastic support, it took only a few months to convince their father to invest in launching a nationwide venture, allowing all branches of their firm to begin serving their cities. They'd started small with just hosting family-friendly fundraisers and giving back seventy to eighty percent of the money earned to communities—orphanages, homeless shelters, and the like—and then widened the circle, helping proficient but poor high school seniors into their local colleges.

He knew America loved what he was doing because Alvarez Consultants had been catapulted from being a multi-millionaire company to making several times that amount per month in their Florida headquarters alone. He still wondered if his father was really pleased with how he led the business that he'd sacrificed so much to build. He had never said so.

Camryn wasn't done, though. He had more to give— much more. If he could take Alvarez Consultants to space, he would. For now, though, he would settle for his goal of going international.

Paige Lewis's voice climbed into the ballad's climax, and he noted the swiveling heads and awed stares that some of the guests were giving her with smug satisfaction. When he'd heard from his manager of music counseling that Paige was one of the few up-and-coming black female artists in Florida, he'd pounced on the opportunity to feature her in at least most of the work functions the company would be hosting that year. It would boost her career and get her more traffic. Also, he liked her style—diverse and modish with a classy spin.

Those were the words he wanted Alvarez Consultants to be associated with.

In the corner of his eye, he saw the flashes. He heard the snaps of several cameras as they captured Paige in her beaded jewel neckline dress that brushed her calves.

"Camryn Alvarez, is that you?"

He turned when he heard a female voice purr his name.

The woman was impressively tall, with gleaming blonde hair smoothed behind her ear in a slick, wet look. He squinted at her cat-like eyeliner as he struggled to focus on her face in the slowly whirling lights circling the dance floor. He had opted out of his contact lenses for the night, thinking that he wouldn't need them. "Do we know each other?" he inquired.

She laughed throatily. The feline eyes. The smirking mouth. Everything about her was cat-like. He didn't like it. "Have you forgotten me already?" She pouted as she draped her arms over his shoulders, presumptuously pulling him into the band of dancing bodies. "It's Julia. Julia Flores."

Camryn's mouth tightened as he reluctantly assented to dancing with her, placing his hands lightly on her waist. Yes, he had already forgotten her, and he couldn't wait to forget her again. He'd met enough girls like Julia to know that they usually wanted one of two things from him: his money or his name—sometimes both. He refused to give his heart to a woman who wanted anything more than his heart. He wouldn't make the same mistake twice.

They swayed together in silence for a few moments, Camryn looking at anything but her. The music would have calmed him entirely if it weren't for the woman in his arms.

"Camryn..." She was looking at him with bright eyes as Paige's voice descended ever lower, the music dropping to a barely audible note. "I'd love to see you again—"

"Wow!" Camryn released her in a flash with a relieved, breathless sigh as his father's voice rang out from the front of the room, rescuing him from whatever words she had almost said.

Breathing out that it had been a pleasure to meet her, he turned to the stage. It wasn't true, but the fact that he'd likely never meet her again soothed his slighted conscience.

The lights flickered back on, illuminating the audience with a warm glow. The teardrop-shaped jewels dripping from a large chandelier hanging from the marbled ceiling above winked shimmering light at him as he brushed through the crowd to get to the stage. He smiled good-naturedly at the shoulder thumps he got from the men and the amiable, some-times demure, smiles he got from the women.

"Now, where's that son of mine?" His father peered comi-cally into the audience, and the guests laughed in response.

Camryn grinned. Lightly jogging up to the stage, he widened his arms with open hands as if to say, "Here I am!"

Laughter rang around the room again, this time mixed with generous applause.

A young man darted from behind the curtain and onto the stage, fixing Camryn's microphone with experienced hands. Turning to the audience, he said, "Good evening, ladies and gentlemen."

A brief laugh broke from Camryn's lips when, after several silent, awkward moments, the delivery girl's mouth started opening and closing in a fish-like manner.

Finally, she said, "Camryn."

His eyebrows knitted together. "Do we know each other?" he asked. She'd said his name so familiarly. He didn't think they'd met before, though. He had seen more beautiful women than he could count, but none with the quiet kind of beauty she had—so beautiful that once it was seen in her almond-shaped eyes and swooping cheekbones, it was hard to forget.

A lovely pink blush suffused those cheeks then. "Oh, no," she stuttered, tucking a stray strand of brown hair from her face. "Well, I know you, obviously. You don't know me."

I would like to, he thought. He paused, hesitating. She was obviously a fan, and he'd never allowed himself to get involved with one of them. Was he even ready to be involved with anyone after Clare? He couldn't deny the magnetic pull he felt toward her, even though he'd been in her presence for barely a minute. "Maybe we should change that." A nerve quickened in his throat. He ignored it. "Do you want to come inside?"

Her fingers tapped against the pizza boxes in her hands, and she wrinkled her nose cutely. "I'm not really allowed to enter customers' homes. It's against company rules."

He nodded understandingly but said, "Not even for a tip? I forgot to tip you when I was paying over the phone." He had fifty dollars in the back pocket of his jeans—he always tipped generously—but he wasn't going to tell her that.

She wavered for a moment, then sighed. "I guess a few minutes wouldn't hurt anyone." She paused with one foot under the doorway, meeting his eyes. He sucked in his breath. Her eyes were deep brown with green and golden undertones, framed by long, silken lashes that were a few shades lighter than her chestnut hair. "You're not going to kill me, are you?"

The words snapped him out of his reverie. He laughed at the very idea. "Kill you? Why on earth would I do that? Are you delivering me burned pizza?" he joked.

She laughed. "Maybe I'm being a little paranoid."

He stared at her for a moment and thought she was the most beautiful woman he'd ever met. "Maybe." The smile remained on his face as he pushed the door closed after her.

Adjusting his glasses, he regretted for a moment that he'd put them on just before answering the door. Both his PA and stylist insisted that he looked considerably better with them off. He hadn't had a choice, though. He'd taken a day off of work to unwind after the intimate party he'd had for new investors the previous night and left his contact lenses in the city in his penthouse.

"Wow." She gasped as they approached the short hallway that led to the kitchen. When he turned to her, her eyes were wide as they took in the cavernous entrance, the curved staircase, and the gilded balcony above. "I don't think I've ever been in a house this big before."

Her hands brushed over the gleaming, dark wooden banister. Camryn worried at his lower lip for a moment. He was drawn inexplicably to this woman. He wanted to know if her personality was as appealing as her beauty. What if she, like the rest, would want him only for his money and fame? He shook his head. There was no guarantee that she would want him at all. He could only have those questions answered by getting to know her.

"A little bit traditional, a little modern." He nodded, smiling at her. It was precisely what he'd been going for when he got the place renovated. "Is this original to the house?" She faced him, her hand still on the banister. It was cool inside, and the air around her carried gentle floral notes.

Before thinking to respond, he had to cough, his mind slow to catch up with what had come out of her mouth—her cupid-bow mouth.

"Is there something on my face?" Her hands tightened on the boxes, and her ponytail swished off of her shoulder as she flicked her hair back.

His ears felt hot. He was being ridiculous. He was thirty-two years old—a grown man, way too old to be blushing over a woman he'd just met. "Oh, no. I was just thinking. The kitchen's this way." He took the two boxes of pizza from her and led her through the short hallway into the kitchen, her simple flip-flops slapping the white marble tiles underfoot. "I left a few old-house charm touches when I was renovating this place, like the stairway," he said, answering her question.

He glanced over his shoulder to find her brushing the dark wood wainscoting with a delicate hand. "Most people don't notice details like that."

Her hand returned to her side, swinging slightly as she walked. "I don't watch much TV, but when I do, I usually watch renovation shows. I find them interesting."

He filed that small detail into his mind, wanting to learn so much more about her. "Why?" he asked.

She mulled it over as they walked into the kitchen, her eyes perusing the spacious area with such curiosity that her eyes lit up. "I think it's the fact that something so old can be made... relevant, present—you know, with a little help. I feel like I've always been that way." She shrugged, her gaze averted from his.

He was quiet for a moment, watching her. "I think I know what you mean," he said quietly. She turned with a surprised expression, and he gave her a slight smile. "Sometimes I feel like I was born in the wrong place at the wrong time."

The sound of a cheering crowd filled the room, and her silky ponytail swung as she peered through the cased opening to the living room.

"Wow," she said. "That is hands down the biggest TV I have ever seen."

His smile widened as he set the pizza boxes on the countertop. His TV was pretty big, dwarfing even the wide electric fireplace beneath it. It was off now, but he'd had many date nights with its blue, artificial flames lighting the place. His chest tightened, and he turned back to the pizza. His mouth watered when he opened the boxes, and the delicious smell of spicy pepperoni wafted through the room.

He turned, munching on a bite, when she suddenly groaned. "This wasn't their best game, was it?" She shook her head, frowning as the Yankees' Corey Kluwer pitched a ball that veered inches too wide from the hitter. The entire crowd groaned in unison, mirroring her, and Camryn couldn't help but laugh.

It was his second time watching the game since it aired the previous night, and saying it "wasn't their best game" was putting it mildly. He'd first watched it with his friend Rylan the previous night, who'd since driven back to the city. Rylan had repeated time and time again that he felt like he was watching a high school game rather than a major league, world-class team playing.

"You watch baseball?" If she answered in the positive, he might just propose.

She turned to him with an affronted expression. "Of course I do. I am a true American."

She joined him when he burst out laughing. "Most people," he said, grinning, "would argue that football is America's game." He had nothing against football, but he would choose baseball over it any day of the week.

"Most people," she said with a playful smile, "would be wrong. Anyway, baseball is decades older than football."

He set his slice of pizza back into the box as his heart picked up. Pizza, a baseball game playing in the background, and a baseball-loving woman smiling at him. Was he dreaming? "My dad has been trying to force-feed me facts like that since I could walk. I don't know if loving baseball is genetic, but if it is, I definitely got it from him."

She rounded the edge of the counter, leaning on top of it.

"Have a slice," he offered, gesturing to the box of pizza.

Her eyes flickered in a moment of hesitation. He mentally willed her to go for it and stay a little longer. She did. "I'm going to regret this so much when I'm looking at the scale tonight." He laughed with her and let his gaze wander down her body. *I doubt that,* he thought. She was tall, though still several inches shorter than his six and a half feet. Her high-waisted jeans hugged her thin waist and curvy hips perfectly. "So, do you play?" His eyes snapped up at her amused gaze.

He reached for his own pizza with burning ears. "Play what?" He realized after the dreaded words left his mouth that she meant baseball, obviously. He cleared his throat. Was it getting hot in here? "Oh, yeah. Since I was a kid. I even played in college. How do you know so much about baseball, anyway? The only person I know who sprouts nerdy facts about it is my dad."

She raised a brow at him with laughing eyes. "Nothing about me is nerdy." She swung onto her heels, her ponytail brushing past her shoulders. He had to agree. "When I'm interested in something, I always want to know as much about it as possible." A faint flush tinged her cheeks, and she looked away from him almost guiltily.

He frowned. Why would she feel guilty?

Her gaze landed on his wrist, where his digital watch flashed the time. As the audience on the TV cheered again, she suddenly gasped, widening her eyes. "Oh, no! I'm late! Not again." Without turning, she bolted for the door.

"Wait," he heard himself cry out, but wait she did not.

As his front door slammed shut with a bang, he let his palm fall on his face. He hadn't even gotten her name.

Caught in the Act

IT HAD TAKEN STELLA NEARLY AN HOUR TO FINALLY fall asleep the previous night. The events of earlier that day had kept whirling through her mind, enveloping her like a wave when she least expected them to. A handsome, funny wave that loved baseball and made her stomach do flips. She'd been surprised to find out that Camryn liked baseball. It was nice to know that there were things about him that she hadn't found in magazine articles—things that she could learn from him as she got to know him.

Not that there was any hope of her getting to know him now. When he'd called out for her as she ran for work, she hadn't stopped to think. He didn't even have her number. She knew where he lived, but no, she couldn't go back now. He probably only saw her as a fan anyway.

She'd worried that her family would see the little smiles she kept indulging herself in as she cooked dinner and as she sorted whatever laundry they'd neglected to put in their washing baskets. But they hadn't noticed. For the first time, she was satisfied with the bit of attention they gave her. She wasn't all that sure about Mackenna, but she was sure to the bone that Julia and Kiana wouldn't hesitate to kill just to have Camryn.

As she veered her scooter left onto Harbor Lane, making her way to Lakewood General Hospital, she wondered what she would say to Robin, her best friend. The light flashed red, and she slowed to a stop, her scooter rumbling begrudgingly beneath her. Robin had been the unwilling recipient of all the daydreams and what-ifs that Stella had ever had about Camryn. She knew she would be happy for her, even if all that happened was her meeting her celebrity crush instead of marrying him like she'd always dreamed.

Maybe she shouldn't say anything at all. Her lips spread into a grin. There was no way Robin wouldn't notice. She had the all-seeing eyes of an owl. Nothing ever missed her notice. She was the best new entry surgeon in Naples, Florida, after all, with a shiny trophy to prove it. They had met four years ago, when Robin was still doing her residency. Robin had just started volunteering at the hospital where her parents died. A year had passed at that point, and the memories she'd had of them were beginning to fade. She had thought that being where they were in their last days would help her deal with the grief and guilt that came with forgetting.

BEEP BEEP BEEP went the mechanical traffic light.

Stella started, fumbling clumsily for the handles and then giving them a firm twist. The light had turned green without her noticing. Her scooter shot forward powerfully, and she gave a wild gasp and then laughed nervously when she reined back control. The driver on her right glared at her through the window. Stella snapped her attention back to the road, turning left from Hastings Street toward the hospital.

She parked her scooter in the workers' parking lot—technically, she wasn't allowed to do this, but no one had ever tried to stop her, so she continued to do so. She padlocked her helmet to the neck of the bike and, after making sure the scooter wouldn't topple over, walked toward Robin. She was waiting for her in her blue scrubs in front of the workers' entrance.

"You're late," she said in greeting, her copper coil-like hair ruffling in the slight breeze. "As usual. Hopefully, your coffee isn't too cold."

Stella's mouth fell open. "As usual?" she repeated. "That's not true at all. I make every effort to be on time."

Robin hummed as her mouth curled into a smile. "That last part may be true, Ads, but you're late at least most of the time. You just have very little awareness of how time works."

Stella frowned. "Just because I'm always late doesn't mean I'm..." She trailed off.

"Always late?" Robin's shoulders shook with laughter.

The automatic doors slid open for them, and Stella shivered as the smell of the hospital, bleachy and metallic, accosted her. She knew most of the hospital's layout like the back of her hand, but there were some things she would never get used to, like how white, bright, and cold it was. Why did they have to use fluorescents? Why couldn't they use different lights with a warm, happy glow?

"If you must know..." Stella gave her friend a mock glare. "I'm only late because I was getting us donuts. Since you clearly don't want them, I guess I'll just have to eat your coffee-caramel, sprinkled donuts. That's the last time I do anything nice for you," she joked.

Robin's eyes lit up, and she gave Stella a side hug, trying not to spill the coffee on either one of them. "You're a superstar, you know that?"

Stella's cheeks warmed at the word superstar, and she looked down at the comfortable trainers she wore for her hospital visits. Their blue and green contrasted cheerily against the white-washed tiles. "I know," she answered, wondering how she would begin the conversation about Camryn, "but I love to hear it."

Robin cocked her head up at her as they walked past the receptionist, and each gave her a little half-wave in greeting. Stella was a few inches taller than Robin and more petite. "Are you okay?" she asked her. "You look a little flushed."

Stella's flush deepened. The words stumbled over each other in her mind as she wondered what to tell her first. "Actually," she began, "there might be something I need to tell you."

They walked through the double-door entrance to the hospital cafeteria, the strong, energizing smell of coffee flooding Stella's senses. After sitting down at one of the tables, Robin said, "I'm all ears."

Stella took a small sip of her coffee and then made a face. "It's tepid."

"Whose fault is that?" Robin arched a brow at her and then closed her eyes with a satisfied groan as she bit into the donut.

Stella deadpanned at her and then said, "Stevie's has a discount for those this week. Four for 10 bucks."

"Okay. You know I can't eat more than two of these per month, or I gain a hundred pounds." Robin lowered her eyebrows suspiciously. "Didn't you say you had something to tell me?"

Her shoulders slumped. "Fine, but don't freak out."

She recounted the events of the previous day to her friend —how it had been a typical Monday morning doing her Uber Eats rounds when she suddenly found herself having a casual conversation about interior design and baseball with Camryn Alvarez. Robin put a hand over her open mouth, the sunlight streaming through the window coloring her eyes in honey tones. "No way!" she exclaimed. "Are you sure you didn't dream it up?"

Stella laughed. "Seriously?"

"What?" Robin said defensively. "You have had dreams about him before." She shook her head, using a napkin to wipe her mouth. "This is insane."

Stella gave a shrug and laughed again. "I know."

"Look at you trying to act all casual! I know you're totally freaking out on the inside," Robin said.

Stella covered her face with her hands, her shoulders shaking with laughter. "I can't believe this actually happened to me." She looked across the table at Robin, reaching for her lukewarm coffee. "It was amazing—while it lasted anyway. I'm probably never going to see him again."

"What?" Robin's voice pealed through the large cafeteria. The few other people in the room turned to look at them. Leaning forward, she said in a normal tone, "What do you mean?"

"I mean, I couldn't stay long enough for us to exchange numbers or anything like that. It's okay, though." It wasn't, not really. She took a big gulp of her now-cold coffee. It tasted gross, but she couldn't bear the thought of Robin buying her Starbucks coffee only for it to be thrown away.

Robin shook her head violently, her springy hair bouncing every which way. "No way, Stella." Her voice was firm. "I totally saw a movie just like this. Fate brought you two together. You just need to believe that it will bring you together again. If you don't believe, who will do it for you?"

Stella rummaged inside her messenger bag for her keys as she ran up the driveway from where she'd parked her scooter on the sidewalk. Her conversation with Robin had taken a little longer than she'd expected. She only got to speak with two of her regular patients before she had to leave again. With the party coming up in just a couple of days, it would be some time before she could go back to the hospital. Eleanor hadn't officially asked yet, but she knew she would be expected to help set up the party.

She'd forgotten her license on her way out earlier and couldn't start her shift until she had it with her. While she was working, she occasionally drove past traffic cops. She didn't want to take her chances of getting pulled aside for a regular license and being found wanting. She couldn't afford tickets. She wasn't late for work, at least. There was still some time left before the restaurants started pinging her Uber profile for deliveries.

She was only a little surprised to find the door unlocked. After a sudden boost in business that Eleanor's boutique had received some months back, she'd gotten a few more employees to man the cash register and help customers with fittings. Julia and Kiana often opted to stay home or leave work early. Mackenna still had full days because she was the only accountant.

Their voices echoed from the kitchen as Stella passed the threshold, closing the door with a quiet click. She paused at the stairway when she heard Camryn's name.

"I met him again." It was Julia's voice, sounding conspiratorial.

Her pulse thrummed at her neck. Before she knew it, she was creeping toward the kitchen, wincing at the tap-tap of her shoes against the tiles. She knew eavesdropping was wrong, but she needed to hear what Julia was about to say.

Kiana gasped. "What! When?"

Julia was swinging on one of the barstools with bright eyes and a gleeful smirk. "Two nights ago. I snuck into some kind of party his company was hosting. I think I remember him saying it was for their latest investors or something."

Kiana was leaning over the countertop, her forgotten half-empty glass of red wine at her side. "How did you even get in?" Her excited smile was marred by the slight twist to her mouth.

"I just pretended I forgot my invite. I was wearing my Louis Vuitton dress, the off-shoulder one with the slitted leg. It only took a little bit of begging to get the guys watching the entrance to let me in."

"Louis Vuitton, off-shoulder..." Kiana gasped. "You witch! You don't have an off-shoulder Louis Vuitton! You stole my dress."

Stella's mouth fell open. Julia and Kiana had been trying to infiltrate Camryn's inner circle for years. That Julia had worn Kiana's dress while speaking to Camryn Alvarez without her was a knife in the back.

A sudden, bitter wave of jealousy rolled over Stella. She tried to swallow it down. She and Julia were more or less the same height, but the similarities ended there. Stella started to carry her weight in her hips more than she had in the past as the years went by. Julia, on the other hand, looked like a supermodel, all long legs and strawberry-blonde hair. She even had dimples. How many girls like Julia did Camryn see daily? It wasn't fair.

"It doesn't even matter." Julia rolled her eyes at her sister, not looking the slightest bit sorry. "He barely had the time for me. He couldn't get away fast enough." She nursed her glass of white wine with unfocused eyes, a frown creasing her brows.

Stella was still watching Julia when Kiana suddenly said, "Stella? What are you doing?"

Kiana had her own glass of wine in hand now, hovering halfway to her mouth, looking at Stella with barely concealed contempt. Mortified, she stepped away from the threshold opening up to the kitchen. She hoped the flush stinging her cheeks didn't show too much. Her mind reeled for a response.

"I— well, I thought I left my license here. Yes, that's right." She nodded violently. "I came back because I needed my license. I heard you guys talking in here and didn't want to interrupt you. I know you work so hard and rarely get time to rest," she flattered.

Kiana's sneer was gone, but Julia was eyeing her suspiciously.

"That is true." Kiana was examining her inch-long artificial nails with eyes framed by superiorly arched brows.

Stella breathed an inaudible sigh of relief. She made a show of searching the kitchen counter with her eyes. "I don't think it's in here. I'll go check in my room." Without waiting for a response, she spun on her heel and beelined for the stairs.

She hated lying, and her conscience smote her fiercely for it as she made her way to the attic, her room. What else could she have said, though? That she was eavesdropping because she had a crush on Camryn Alvarez and that she had met him — and he hadn't tried to run away from her? That he'd ever wanted to speak more with her? They would never forgive her, even if it wasn't her fault that he hadn't tried to avoid her.

A smile took possession of her lips. Even if Camryn Alvarez wasn't interested in her in the same way she was interested in him, at least he didn't hate her. Not at all. A memory unraveled itself free in her mind of Camryn, calling out for her to wait as she ran back to work. Her smile widened.

Maybe Robin was right. Perhaps fate would bring them together again.

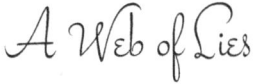

CAMRYN LEANED HIS HEAD BACK AGAINST THE couch, the leather cooling the back of his neck. His whole body felt hot. He tugged at his tie until it was hanging loosely from his neck, like he'd done with his uniform in his private school days. All day, it had felt like a noose around his neck.

The day had passed in a blur. He couldn't get out of the office fast enough today. He started feeling despair that he would never see her again.

Her. That's all he could call her. Every time he remembered that he hadn't asked for her name—which was often— he felt like an idiot all over again. And rightly so, he would think to himself. He would never find her.

After she left two days ago, when he was in his country home, he'd done the only thing he could do: make more orders with his Uber Eats app for hours. All that had gotten him was enough food to feed a small village. No beautiful girl. He'd detoured to an orphanage that his firm supported to drop the food off on the way to work.

The same man had made all the deliveries. He'd lost count of how many he made—each time, handing him his food with an increasingly incredulous expression. It had almost made him laugh. Almost.

A part of his mind kept rolling eyes at him over how ridiculous he was being. She was just a girl.

And yet, she wasn't. He couldn't remember a single time he had spoken so casually, so normally with a woman, except with family, of course. Every single one of the women he'd been with had been wealthy and at least moderately well-known. His delivery girl had shown up in jeans and flip flops; his past girlfriends had always had pearls and diamonds dripping from their necks and ears and heels long enough to impale a man.

He hadn't had any choice over which family he'd been born into, so he was well aware of how fortunate he was to have never wanted for anything. In fact, that was one of his most significant motivating factors for working hard. Nothing brought him more joy than seeing people who had so little finally have not just enough to survive but to actually live.

And yet, he couldn't shake the feeling that meeting her was the luckiest thing that had ever happened to him.

His phone buzzed. The sound cut through the rumbling of traveling cars outside his penthouse and the low buzz coming from his TV. The sun was beginning to set outside, bathing the city in fiery oranges and yellows. The late afternoon light flooded into his living room and open-plan kitchen. Camryn straightened slowly, tugging his phone out of his pocket. It was a text from Stan.

STAN

We found her.

He jerked upright, his heart hammering against his chest. He'd begrudgingly told his PA about meeting a girl he couldn't stop thinking about when he had pulled him aside at the end of the day, wondering why he'd been in such a foul mood. He had even been a little short with his managers. He would apologize to them tomorrow. When Stan asked for his phone and took it to the IT department, he hadn't expected anything helpful to come out of it.

But they'd found her. His thumbs hovered over the screen as he tried to catch his brain up to what was happening.

> What do I do?

Three bubbles popped up, and Camryn tapped his foot as he waited, worrying at his lower lip.

STAN

> Nothing. We called in favor with Uber headquarters. She's coming right now.

He stared at the text with wide eyes, the sound blaring from the TV turning into white noise in his ears. Another text came through:

STAN

> ;)

The winking emoji was enough to snap him out of it. He raced to his bedroom, bare feet slapping against the floor, throwing off his tie and then his shirt and pants as he ran to the back of the penthouse. If she was coming, he'd want to look like himself, and there was nothing he hated more than wearing a suit and tie. He was going to have to give Stan another raise. That man was constantly saving his life.

Some minutes passed as he slipped into dress pants and a simple white t-shirt. The elevator dinged, and he shrugged at the rows of shoes peering up at him, opting to go barefoot.

The distance from his bedroom to the elevator seemed to have stretched oceans longer while he was getting ready. He punched in the security code on the cool monitor, its screen a blue-white light in the warm glow of his apartment. His heart was at his throat. The elevator doors swung slowly and smoothly open.

All the breath in his lungs was swept away when he saw her. She was in a pink sundress that hugged her waist snugly and fluttered to her knees; her brown hair coiled to the side in a thick brown braid that spilled over her shoulder. His chest felt tight. "It's you."

Stella smiled her brightest smile. It was probably her last customer of the day—the sun was setting, and Tuesdays were always slower than other days. She'd received absolutely zero tips, and one of her customers' dogs had chased her all the way out of his gate while he laughed. It hadn't been the best day for her. It was nice to have her last customer be so polite.

She squinted at him from the harsh light of the chrome-faced elevator. His body was outlined by a dim glow, which embraced the apartment behind him, and his hair was a messy tangle crowning his head.

"Good evening, sir. How can I help you?" she said, hovering in the elevator as the man continued to stand in place. She wasn't precisely sure why she was here, except that management had informed her in-app that a customer had had a problem with his order, and she would have to be the one to help him. She wasn't allowed to enter the actual apartment—company rules. Her mind wandered against her will to Camryn and his insistence that she enter his home.

"You don't remember me?" The words snapped her back to the present. He took one step forward, and the elevator light reflected his crestfallen face.

"Camryn!" She gasped.

A smile spread across his face. "Maybe today I'll actually learn your name."

"Maybe you will," she replied, smiling back at him.

She didn't resist when he motioned her into the apartment. "Wow," she breathed. An entire wall of wide-open glass doors gave her a panoramic view of Naples like she had never seen before. She didn't know what to say.

Her head swiveled to find Camryn watching her. "Come and see." He guided her onto the large balcony. "It's one of the best views in the city."

She stepped out into the cool evening, the breeze catching a few strands of her hair that had managed to escape her braid. Something glassy and dark blue reflected the handful of bright stars that could be seen in the dark, chasing the sun away. With a start, she realized that it was a swimming pool, curving all the way around the balcony. A trail cut around the pool to the edge of the building, and Camryn guided her along it.

"What do you think?" he asked her.

Dusk shadowed the world around her, and one by one, the lights of city buildings flickered on like fireflies. The stars above them smiled secretly down at her as if they knew that this was the loveliest night of her life. "It's beautiful. I couldn't imagine getting to wake up to this every day."

"Sunrises are even better, believe it or not." He was looking down at her with a relaxed smile gracing his firm mouth. She had seen every commercial with him in it and read every article concerning him and his firm. Still, she had never seen him look at anything the way he was looking at her. "Maybe you'll get to see them one day."

A moment passed, and Stella's eyes widened.

"Wait," he said, straightening, "that came out wrong."

She hugged her arms around herself, wondering how many women he'd brought onto this balcony. How many women would be brought onto this balcony after? Her mind searched for something, anything to say, as he rubbed a tired hand over his face. "What did you need help with? I can't stay very long," she said. "I have a party to plan."

He gave her a sheepish grin and scratched the back of his neck. "I kind of might have gotten Uber Eats to get me... well, you."

Stella stiffened. Half of her was flattered that he'd tried to find her, especially after she thought she'd never see him again. The other half of her was wondering if he always got what he wanted. She wasn't sure which side was winning until a dark strand of hair fell onto his forehead. Her hand itched to brush it back.

"So you do party planning?" he asked.

"Yeah, I guess." She shrugged.

"Ah." He melted against the railing again, angling his body toward hers. "I thought this was your only job."

All at once, she realized her mistake. He meant if she was an actual party planner, not a twenty-eight-year-old who still lived with her family and worked for Uber Eats, of all things, as her only source of income. A sudden wave of shame slammed into her, and she couldn't look at him anymore. She had never been embarrassed, no matter what job she had. Her family had never been wealthy. Stella had sometimes operated the cash register in the small bookshop her dad ran. Her mother had been a housewife. How could she explain that she was twenty-eight years old and still had nothing of import to show for her life? How could she explain it to him, one of the most ambitious and resourceful people in the world?

Maybe she wouldn't have to.

"Well," she heard herself saying, looking down at the

disjointed streams of cars curving the building on the road below, "I do a little bit of this and that. Party planning, and now this new gig I got myself with Uber Eats."

"Tell me more." She snuck a glance at him, and a million butterflies took flight at his bright eyes and the slight smile edging his lips.

Her hands were gripping so tightly onto the railing that she felt them begin to go numb. "Uber Eats is relatively new to the area." That was true. She'd only started working for them a few months ago. "So I reached out to them to give them a little local know-how and help them get local drivers and the like."

"So you're basically partnering with Uber Eats, Naples?"

Her hair fell over her face when she looked down at her feet, bobbing her head yes. Every one of her toes glared up at her with an accusatory red gleam. Liar. Would the stars still be smiling at her when she looked up?

"That is amazingly impressive, for lack of a better word." A hand brushed over her shoulder as he drew her hair back, erupting goosebumps across her skin. "I mean that."

She looked up at him. The stars lit up the night, aided by the artificial lights from the buildings surrounding them. She had never thought of gray eyes as warm. One day, the lie she told him would weigh on her shoulders with the mass of all the mountains in the whole world, but for right now, it was worth it, just for the way he looked at her.

The next day whirled past in a fit of animal print wallpaper and paper mâché.

Stella's aunt had hired some men to fill the small warehouse she'd rented with gleaming opal chairs—also rented—a makeshift stage, and large vases that she'd told her she planned to fill with "white and periwinkle delphiniums". If Stella had been preparing this place for the fashion collection launch, she would have gone with dark reds, dark blues, and lots of steel. An industrial-themed setup would work perfectly with dark cement floors.

Eleanor had had weeks to plan for this party. She didn't understand why she had waited until the very last day to piece the details together.

Stella had already stuck the leopard print wallpaper onto the red galvanized copper walls, with her aunt's frantic gaze and sharp mouth constantly at her heels. The emerald-colored carpet Eleanor had picked out was laid against the stage. Tomorrow night, models would be sauntering across its grassy texture to the stage from outside, where she was currently shaping rustic bowls out of gluey paper mâché.

Kiana, beside her, was painting the dried bowls in bold pinks and blues.

Someone had cleared the ground around the warehouse by several feet, but untouched heads of wheat waved all around her under the gentle breeze. She almost began to enjoy herself until she looked up and spotted her aunt yawping at a man in a blue work suit. He was shrinking away from her with wide eyes. Stella almost laughed. He towered at least a head above her and still looked like he was about to bolt in terror. Whatever she was shouting at him about reached her muffled and muted by the breeze.

Kiana's snicker cut through the squelch of Stella's hands as they squeezed together against the gloppy clumps of paper in the large bowl set on the table. Stella watched as Kiana laughed at the altercation between Eleanor and the man. Then she looked back down at her task, wondering how life would have been for her if her parents were still alive. Even the good memories she had of them—the ones where her mother wasn't sick and her father wasn't dying—made her sad.

Their work was completed hours after the sun was swallowed by the horizon. The only sound that filled the warehouse was the swishing of the broom as she swept away the dust. Her aunt and cousins had left her to do this one last task after the workers left, entrusting Stella and her faithful scooter to get her back home. Only a few lights were on, but she could see well enough that they'd done an okay job getting the place ready.

Camryn would be here tomorrow night, watching as strings of gorgeous women prowled up and down the stage in skimpy, animal-print clothes. The thought hit her like a truck. She thought of the suspicion in Julia's eyes a few days ago after she was caught eavesdropping. It would be better for her if she weren't here. Her cousins, she knew, wouldn't hesitate to put her on trial for the lies she'd told Camryn if they found out.

In Vogue

A SLOW TRICKLE OF PEOPLE STARTED TO STREAM into the warehouse as the sunset painted the wispy sky shades of lavender and baby blue.

Stella watched from the side entrance as the seats slowly filled with the social elite of Naples. She spotted only one face that she recognized—Chara Roberts. She was in a triangular, snowy white dress that haltered at her chest and flared out to her calves. She was a fashion reporter, whom Stella had heard Kiana gush over more than once this season for her work at the Paris women's fashion week.

A low buzz filled the cavernous space as the guests faced one another in their seats, leaning forward to converse. The brilliant lights overheard were centered in the middle of the warehouse, where the stage, seats, and furniture were. The wainscoted animal print flashed luminescently from the dark walls of the warehouse. Eleanor had chosen the transparent chairs fittingly. They shimmered inconspicuously in the lighting, brightening the cavernous warehouse. The grass-like carpet rippled from the side of the stage to the side entrance, which Stella was peering through. Royal blue vases holding odorless white and periwinkle flowers were scattered in the space in front of the stage.

Stella stepped back sheepishly when she spotted Julia looking at her with a curl to her lip across from her, her body also angled toward the warehouse. "Why are you even still here, Stella?" She said her name like it left a bad taste in her mouth. Her thin, high cheekbones were iridescent with glitter, which complemented the leopard print dress she was wearing. A line of models trailed behind her from two minivans whose headlights were blinking in Stella's eyes.

Squinting at Julia, she said, "You're right." She was the last person Stella ever wanted to anger. Stella and Mackenna could make her life difficult whenever the fancy took them. Still, Julia was diabolical enough to make Stella's life miserable. "I see your mom right over there. I'll ask her."

She plodded over to her aunt. "Eleanor, everything looks amazing."

Eleanor faced her with a pleased but unsurprised expression, arching her brows slightly and smirking. The rumble of the minivans cut off.

"Unless there's anything else you need me to do, can I get going before the sun goes down?" After a pause, she added, "I know you have some photographers out tonight; I wouldn't want to distract anyone by accidentally getting into one of the pictures." If Eleanor thought Stella's presence would somehow endanger the night, she might be more willing to let her leave.

Eleanor's thumbs hovered over her phone as her gaze swept over Stella's messy ponytail, her faded baseball tee, and her years-old trainers. "Sweetheart, you couldn't do that even if you tried."

Stella's face stung with a hot blush. She opted to say nothing in response. It wasn't like she had been trying to look good tonight. She was only here as support to help with small details like sweeping and mopping the warehouse's floor again. She had been hovering uselessly for almost half an hour. Robin was back to her regular day shifts, and Stella had been hoping to have a girl's night with her tonight.

"No." Eleanor looked down at her phone. "You'll stay here. My caterer isn't responding to my texts, so I might need you to drive over to town if we run out of finger foods or wine. My car keys are in the blue minivan. If she doesn't respond, I'll send you a text." She leveled a glare at her. "Make sure to check your phone, okay?"

"I will," Stella replied with a sinking heart, her expression falling as soon as her aunt turned her back to her. She watched Eleanor approach the models, her long heels sinking into the ground with every step.

It looked like the evening was about to begin. A handful of waiters were hovering at the edge of the hundred or so chairs set in two groups of fifty seats each. Some refilled empty glasses, and others placed delicate-looking canapés on the guests' plates.

The lights dimmed, directing every eye to the lit stage just as a hush blanketed the audience. It was so quiet that if she hadn't been looking into the warehouse, she would've thought that everyone had suddenly disappeared. Julia and Kiana, the front most models in the line, craned their necks into the warehouse.

Stella's heart flopped clumsily inside her chest. She knew he had arrived without even seeing him.

Without waiting to consider whether it was wise or not, she stumbled to the entrance. Similarly, she peered into the warehouse, standing across from her cousins.

Camryn's footsteps resounded as he walked to the cluster of seats on the left of the stage with an easy, loping gait, looking as if he were taking a stroll through a park—not at all bothered by the hundred heads that swiveled in his direction as he passed by. He slinked into a seat in the very last row and turned to the woman beside him with a nod and a heart-achingly handsome smile. The low hum of conversation from the guests rose again.

He looked so different from the man she had met in an aristocratic manner and from the way he had looked in his penthouse. She liked the Camryn who gushed over baseball and walked barefoot in his house. This Camryn was polished to perfection in his gleaming navy trousers and simple white dress shirt.

"He is so gorgeous." Stella was startled. The two dozen models were now crowded around the door, each trying not to be seen. A woman with bouncy coppery hair in a one-shoulder zebra-striped dress that flared out from her thighs to brush the ground was leaning over her shoulder, looking into the warehouse just as she had been. Stella nodded dumbly in response.

When she looked back into the warehouse, she found him watching her with a small smile, nodding absently at whatever the woman beside him was saying with expressive, gesticulating hands.

She shot back from the door with burning cheeks, earning "heys" when she jostled some of the girls. With a muttered apology, she stumbled toward the wheat field and plopped herself onto the ground. After looking up at the sky as it darkened, she slipped her phone out of her back pocket and checked for messages from Eleanor. But she found none. The night seemed to drag by slowly. It felt like several eons passed as one after the other, the stars blinked into the sky. She looked down at her crumpled shirt. If she'd known she would see Camryn tonight, she would have tried to at least look like a girl.

Behind her, deep, frantic drums boomed with jungle sounds—shrieking monkeys, trumpeting elephants, and snarling leopards—intermingled. Wheat straws bent under her weight as she stretched her legs out, resigning herself to playing a word game on her phone. When the music finally died away to a calm, syncopated legato, a million crickets sang out from the wheat field, having previously been muted by the loud music.

Stella bolted upright. She had no problem with bugs, but she preferred leaving tonight without any of them fixed to her clothes or hair. She slipped her hairband off, combing through her hair with her fingers, and then retied it. No bugs.

The crunch of footsteps and the bristling of heads of grain made her turn. Camryn was artfully weaving through the field, wheat clinging greedily onto his legs.

His arms shone bronze under the moonlight. "Are you wearing body makeup?" she asked, her voice rose so he could hear her over the symphony drifting from the warehouse.

"Maybe. Or maybe it's my inner beauty shouting inwardly?" His white teeth beamed at her in the dark as she laughed. "Have you been out here this entire time?" When he reached her, he brushed his hand down her arm. "Are you cold?" Her baseball shirt covered her skin, but that didn't stop her stomach from fluttering with nerves.

Stella nodded, wrapping her arms around her waist. Being around him made her feel jittery in a way none of her past relationships ever had.

"Well..." He guided her away from the halo of trampled wheat surrounding her with a hand on her back. "I know just the way to warm you right up."

"Where are you taking me?" Stella asked with a laugh, folding the seat belt between her hands in a nervous tic.

"It's a surprise." He grinned, still keeping his eyes on the road, as they took another left turn. "But I promise, you're going to love it."

"I didn't think you knew me well enough to be surprising me." They had only known each other for a handful of days, after all.

"I know that you and I share one thing in common."

"We both have gorgeous hair?" Stella joked.

He gave her a long, lingering look—long enough for her to turn red and start wondering if his lousy driving habits were going to get her killed tonight. "I do have gorgeous hair. Thanks for noticing."

She gave an exasperated laugh. "That's not what I said, and you know it."

His right hand left the steering wheel to give her hand a warm, calloused squeeze. He was very touchy. Remembering the question Mackenna had asked, she now started to wonder to herself how this very handsome, obviously affectionate man had remained single for more than a year now, especially with his name and wealth. "We're here," he announced.

He stopped the car, and Stella looked through the windshield with a soft smile. "An indoor baseball training center." She wasn't even aware that Naples had one.

He opened the door for her, and she fumbled to unfasten her seatbelt, her hands slowed by the shock. With her hand tucked into his arm, they walked to the door. "Isn't it closed?" she asked. "It's pretty late."

A single car drove past with a sickly-sounding engine, illuminating the jingling key that Camryn pulled out of his pocket. His grin shone brightly in the light from the LED sign that blared, "ROGER'S baseball and training center". She turned to look at the street as Camryn opened the door. They weren't in the best part of town. If someone ran around the corner in a ski mask with a butcher knife in hand, she might spot them in time to run. She shook her head, turning back to the door as she heard it ease open. She was paranoid again.

"How do you have the keys for this place?" Stella asked. They walked through a dark hallway with a carpet that Stella suspected was responsible for the musty air.

"I'm always here. This is my happy place whenever work gets too busy or I'm having family problems."

It wasn't much of a surprise that work could get busy for him. He ran a multibillionaire business after all—but that he could have family problems made her wonder. In the dark, she saw the fuzzy outline of him flip a glowing switch. Light drifted toward them from further down the hallway.

"What kind of family problems?" she pried, letting her curiosity get the better of her.

"You know the small skirmishes that happen in families." He gave her a wry smile. She didn't smile back. She only got to see family skirmishes from the outside. "That and worrying about my little brother."

Her eyes snapped to his face. "You have a little brother?" How had she missed this information in the hours that she'd spent scouring the web?

"We don't talk about him much." He raked a slow hand through his hair. "He's a bit of a black sheep. We don't know what's going on with him. Sometimes I suspect that Amelia might know something, but..." He shook his head, his eyes clouded with sadness. "I don't really have any reason to think that."

Amelia Alvarez. She didn't know much about Camryn's sister, just that she was the media and marketing mastermind behind Alvarez Consulting and a fashion icon.

"Amelia's my sister," he said, looking over his shoulder at her when the silence stretched long after his words.

"I know," she replied. At his startled look, she added with

a laugh, "You're kind of famous." And mentally willed him not to think she was a stalker, even though she was.

He laughed to himself and then softly said, "I guess I am." With a sweeping hand, he announced in a louder voice, "Here we are."

"Here" consisted of green turf with wide strips of reed mats in the center of the room, each enclosed by floor-to-ceiling black nets. Benches surrounded the nets, and Camryn emptied his trouser pockets and placed their contents—his phone and the keys he'd used to unlock the door—on one of them.

"I have something to say to you, Stella." He faced her with a sternly set mouth, hands akimbo.

She cocked her head at him and folded her arms, a smile playing about her lips. "What's that?"

He closed the distance between them. Every tendon on her body tightened with intense expectation, waiting for his next move. "Just because you're a cute girl..." His eyes had drifted from her wide eyes to her mouth. "Doesn't mean I'm not going to kick your butt at this." He turned sharply, heading for a zipper in the first row of nets that she only spotted when he started to open it.

Stella was breathing again. "We'll see about that," she called to his back. She followed him in through the open zipper after setting her phone beside his, and then looked around as he closed it after her. A machine was set opposite where they were standing, with a white baseball with its characteristic red yarn set in its tubular opening. Beside her, a bat that gleamed metallically leaned against a large, padded mat beside Camryn.

"Have you ever played?" he asked.

"Maybe once or twice." She shrugged. She had played enough to know that she was terrible. "I've played enough to know that mine isn't the butt that will be getting kicked tonight."

He laughed aloud, hooting, head tilted to the ceiling. "Trash-talking, are we? You surprise me. I thought you were a nice girl."

Stella laughed back. "I only surprise people who can't handle what they dish out."

He winced like she shoved him, and she laughed again. "Okay, let's see what you've got. I'll set the machine and bat first." He walked across the net to the machine. "I don't like to brag, but I'll warn you: I made it to the first team in my freshman year of college baseball and kept playing almost to my last year."

"I don't believe that at all," she called as she leaned back into the padding in a crouch.

"That I played baseball into my last year of college?"

"No, that you don't like bragging." She laughed victoriously.

He bent over the machine, which looked up at her with wide eyes and a mouth threatening a grin. "Was that an evil laugh? Should I be worried for my life?"

It was her turn to laugh with her head thrown back. He laughed softly and shook his head, the machine beeping loudly as he pressed buttons she couldn't see. Being with him was so easy. Meeting Robin had saved her from sinking into a deep depression after her parents died, but being with him wasn't like being rescued; it was like flying weightlessly. A thought brought her down to earth: was he allowed to make her this happy when she was lying to him?

She found something else to look at.

"Getting nervous?" Camryn asked. He was walking back toward her. "Don't worry; I'll go easy on you." She smiled wanly. He reached down to the bat beside her with a frown. "Are you feeling okay? I can drive you back home if you want."

"No!" she said, and then forced herself to perk up. "I'm fine, really."

He squeezed her side. Suddenly, every nerve ending was at the point where his hand touched hers. Her eyes widened. "Okay. If you say so." She felt cold when he stepped away.

Beeps that climbed in pitch rang through the space, and suddenly a ball was whistling toward her face. She didn't even have time to scream. From the corner of her eye, she saw Camryn swing his bat in an arcing flash of black and heard the hard thump as the bat and the ball met. The ball collided with the unyielding net and rolled back onto the pitch.

She and Camryn faced each other with wild eyes and then burst out in laughter. "Oh my gosh! Are you okay?" he forced out as he laughed.

"Thanks to you, I still have a face!"

As the beeping sounded again, she scrambled for the corner of her net and crouched, watching. With his eyes fixed on the ball, he angled his body toward it as it came flying, and then he bent his rear arm, sending the ball flying to the net again. She could do that. She watched his form with unflinching eyes, ball after ball, repeatedly shaking off the thought that the machine was aiming for her face. He didn't miss a single ball.

When her turn came, he took up her position in the corner of the net, leaning onto the balls of his feet to watch her. She mimicked the way he had been standing toe-to-toe.

"Nice form," he said.

She smiled widely. She could do this. When the last beep sounded, she watched the ball until she couldn't watch it anymore. Squeezing her eyes shut while still imitating Camryn's form, she braced for the impact of her bat meeting the ball. The wind whistled by her ear, and her eyes flew open as she turned. The ball hit the net and then rolled back to her feet. Her shoulders slumped.

She couldn't do this.

Camryn laughed softly at her. She shot him a mock glare. "Laughing at your competition isn't being much of a good sport."

"Here, I'll teach you." She didn't know what he meant until his arms were around her and his strong hands were covering hers over the bat. She had never felt so small.

Second beep. Third beep. Was her heart beating? Fourth beep. "Keep your eyes open. Watch the ball." His voice rasped in her ears, and her arms limped, the bat kept up by his hands.

As the ball flew toward them, his body enveloped hers, molding her hands,back, and legs into his own form like potter-shaped clay. She was happy when the bat hit the ball, but being in his arms made her even happier.

Family Night

Camryn eyed the drink Rylan was drinking. It was his third one, and the night was early yet.

Rylan narrowed his angular eyes. "Take a picture, mate. It'll last longer." He finished his invitation with a wink. He had more than a decade of friendship with him, but the Australian accent was still surprising. Well, not surprising per se; it was more like annoyingly cool.

Camryn rolled his eyes. "I thought you were a lawyer, not a model," he replied, mostly to distract Rylan while he caught his own mother's eye. They were in the kitchen with her, with the rest of their two families, getting the board games out so they could choose what to play for the evening. Rylan had been acting weird for weeks now during family game nights. Camryn needed to get a day with him away from their families to just talk.

Rylan's face lit up, and a pleased expression made its way to his face. "It's true. I am a lawyer. And a go—"

"Good one at that. Yes, we know, dear." His mother rounded the counter and snatched Rylan's glass of whiskey from his hand just as his mouth opened for another gulp, giving him a look that silenced whatever complaint was forming in his mouth. "The last time you got drunk in my house, I had to get a new Persian carpet. Do you know how expensive Persian carpets are?"

Both Camryn and Rylan turned beet red at the look she gave them. The fluted, sparkling glasses sang as they bumped into each other when she set them on the counter.

Camryn could count the number of events he'd attended that he remembered detail for detail on his hand. His eighteenth birthday was one of them. Everything from the Katy Perry song blasting from the speakers he'd borrowed from Rylan to Rylan encouraging Camryn to drink by getting so drunk himself that he expelled all the contents of his stomach on his mother's sea blue and metallic silver carpet.

Needless to say, the party slowed to a gradual end after that.

He looked at Rylan. They grinned secretly at each other. Oh, the good old days. Rylan had been horrified when he learned just how much of a "goody-two-shoes" Camryn was. His sister was such a tattletale. Since their freshman days, he'd been trying to get Camryn to do the "wild and wonderful". There were times when he got Camryn into serious trouble, as proven by his mother's spoiled carpet. She'd been mad at him for weeks afterward—but most times, he helped Camryn relax and unwind from his constantly busy life. Usually, through a getaway to some faraway island for a week or two. The previous year, he'd taken him and Amelia to the Caribbean. It was fun.

"I saw that look," his mother murmured without looking up, her long, graying hair tucked behind her ears like she'd done when he was just a kid. These days, her hair was grayer than the auburn Amelia had gotten from her.

He looked at Rylan again, and this time, they shared horrified looks. He loved his mother to bits, and nobody could convince him that she wasn't the most wonderful person on earth to ever exist. Nonetheless, sometimes he wondered if she wasn't secretly a witch or something of the like.

She suddenly looked at him with narrowed eyes. Clearly, she hadn't read his mind, had she? "Let me get that for you, Mom." He scrambled to take one of the trays to the living room, following the voices that drifted toward him. "Are you coming?" he called over his shoulder. Rylan responded with a grunt.

He balanced the tray in one hand, and the hot dogs on it tottered precariously. He paused at the doorway to take in the scene before him. Amelia and Charlotte, Rylan's mom, sat on the edges of two settees that they'd dragged from the other end of the living room to the corner adjacent to the frosted French doors, heads leaning conspiratorially together, whispering fervently. He heard, "Should I pretend to have an Australian accent?" and then, "No, absolutely not. Just be yourself."

Bailey gave him a tight, anxious smile when they noticed him, and Amelia braised him with a look dripping with sisterly scorn, which is very poisonous stuff. He shrugged and approached the leather couch his father was sharing with Rylan's dad. Who, after all, was he to discern the things that happened in a conversation between two women? Greater men had tried and failed.

As he set the tray on one of the side tables framing the couch, Ethan said, "Don't you have some stronger stuff, Cam? Anything to distract me from your father's nonsensical words."

Camryn was torn between laughing at the jab at his dad and frowning over the old nickname. Dad had been trying to convert Ethan into a baseball lover since the day they met. The nickname won. "I'm thirty-two years old," he asserted, throwing himself on his unassigned assigned seat, a suede armchair with sunken buttons that glimmered with real gold.

"No thirty-two-year-old man should be called Cam." He'd been saying this for years. As long as they'd been having family game nights—which was almost as long as he'd known Rylan. No one had yet to listen to him.

"It doesn't matter what you say. I'll always remember you the way you looked when I first met you." Ethan paused to reach over his dad's body to the tray, grabbing a hotdog. "I'm just glad you got a good haircut."

Camryn frowned and brushed the short hair at the back of his head. It was longer at the top. When he was younger, it fell like a windswept mop across his face. Looking at pictures now made him cringe.

It made sense then, though. Growing up under the shadow of the Alvarez name had been demanding. His grades had to be on par with his prowess on the baseball field, or the family name would be tarnished. He'd had to wear ties that pinched his neck almost every two weeks for work functions. Heck, he hadn't even been able to get a pimple without a shadow darkening his father's face.

And he had been a good kid. He never got into fights. Always kept his grades pretty good. Putting his foot down on anyone touching his hair had been liberating, even if present-time him regretted it.

He suddenly thought of Stella. He hadn't stopped thinking about her since their night out at the batting cage. What had she been wearing that night? Trainers, he remembered. Old, beat-up trainers and a pair of faded jeans that hugged every inch of her just right. She'd made even that look good. She wouldn't care about something as minute as a bad hairstyle he'd had ages ago. No, he was sure she wouldn't. Still, though, he wouldn't want her to see him that way. He remembered the look of awe she'd given him after he folded his body around hers and helped her hit the baseball.

Every nerve in his body remembered that look. No, she definitely couldn't find out about that ugly hairdo.

"You okay, Bud?" His father had abandoned the baseball game and was watching him closely.

Uh-oh. His dad never failed to surprise him with how perceptive he was. He hesitated. Was he ready for his dad to know about Stella yet? Was he prepared for anyone to know about her? To him, she was like a diamond that he'd stumbled upon without even looking for it. And yet, there were things that he wanted to know that his dad could tell him—things concerning Stella or women in general. Not knowing what to do, he smiled and shrugged. "I'm starving."

His dad studied him for a moment and then turned back to the TV. He'd probably noticed something—nothing got past his dad—and just decided not to press him on it yet. Camryn heaved a sigh of relief. He couldn't even begin to string the words into a coherent sentence about how a woman he'd known for barely a week had his mind strung around her like a sailor's knot.

"So," his mother began, when the snacks and drinks were all set on the multiple side tables in the living room. Everyone sat around the dark cherry wood coffee table with a glass top. "I suppose this is when we start arguing about which game we're playing for the night."

"I know I say this every time..." Rylan's hands were already raised defensibly. "But I really mean it this time. It's been forever since we played Monopoly."

"It's true," Amelia piped unhelpfully.

Camryn narrowed his eyes at her. "I think we should play Scrabble."

"You always think we should play Scrabble." The words were muffled, spoken around the hotdog Ethan had just taken a bite out of. "You get paid for using words like 'anachronistic' and 'callipygian.' I don't think playing Scrabble against you would be fair."

A general mumble of assent went around the room. Only his dad didn't seem to agree, which wasn't very helpful considering that he was doing the exact same job his father had done. "I have never used the word 'callipygian' in my life. Most people prefer not to speak about large, round, succulent buttocks," Camryn said half-heartedly, leaning back into his couch with folded arms.

"You need to get in better company." Bailey shot her son a look of dismay after Rylan mumbled the words. Camryn bit back a laugh for his own mother's sake.

"That's my point, exactly. 'Callipygian' isn't even a word. I literally just made it up, and you still knew what it meant." A small laugh broke out from Camryn at Ethan's words.

Wanting to avoid a long argument, he said, "Fine. Monopoly then. But 'callipygian' is a word."

After a long game of Monopoly that boosted Rylan and Ethan's confidence—Rylan had won, as he always did when they were playing Monopoly, although Ethan was peacocking solely because Ethan was his son—his mother said, "So, Camryn."

He and Amelia groaned loudly. His father examined his glass of diet cola closely. "No, Mom, I'm not married yet. Just as I wasn't married two weeks ago when you asked."

"That's not what I was going to say. And I'm not trying to set you up either," she said when she saw the look on his face. "I already have."

Camryn shook his head incredulously at his mom.

"You don't even have to worry about it. You'll see her at the gala."

His mom promptly turned to a conversation with Charlotte, who had been watching as Amelia packed the monopoly pieces back into their box. That was it, then. Camryn shook his head at his mom. She was always pulling stunts like this. She'd been worrying about having grandbabies since Camryn was a teenager. This stunt of hers didn't surprise him, though.

He needed to talk with his dad. He'd been agonizing all night over whether or not he should. Still, with his company's annual gala just a week away, he knew that the conversation needed to happen. When he caught his father's eye, he gestured with a slight jerk of the head for the door. He and his dad leaving to have a conversation in the office happened often enough to not draw any attention from the others.

After following him down the brightly lit hallway, he walked through to the office. This was a place that looked the same no matter how old he got. He hadn't been allowed in here until he was in his twenties. It made him feel like a child again, at a place he shouldn't be. He shook the feeling off and slinked into one of two dark leather armchairs angled toward triplet casement windows that opened to a view of a large oak withering yellow leaves gradually in the wind.

"It's a girl," his father said once he'd gotten his old pipe out. He didn't actually smoke it. Camryn thought he just liked having the philosophical air it gave him when giving his son advice. Seeing Camryn eyeing it, he winked, his eyes crinkling into a billion lines around them.

Camryn leaned back into the armchair, resting his neck on its crest. "I met her by chance, really." He explained how he and Stella met on that fateful day when she delivered his food, and then about their second meeting.

"Seems a bit miraculous. Not that you two managed to meet again—the fact that she likes baseball as much as you do."

They both laughed. "So, what should I do? I know that I like her, but I also know that I shouldn't like her as much as I do. I don't know her well enough."

"I can't make this decision for you, son."

Camryn frowned at his father. He'd been trying to micro-manage him since he was in diapers, and now he suddenly couldn't make this decision for him?

Catching his son's look, he laughed and said, "I won't do this for you. I know I drove you crazy when you were younger, trying to make you do and be what I thought was best for you. I'm not going to do that anymore. I just want you to be happy —it's all I've ever wanted for you. So I'm going to let you choose. You've got a solid pair of brain cells in that head, and anyway, I always like your ideas better than I like my own." He winked at him.

Camryn straightened in his seat, suddenly not being able to look at his father anymore. "Thanks, Dad." He cleared his throat. He had noticed a change in his dad but had attributed it to his old man getting older. "You know what happened last time. I let my guard down, and I was completely humiliated." Clare. He still felt a pang in heart when he thought of her. However, he never dared to say it out loud.

"If by humiliated you mean heartbroken, then yes, I remember." He paused. His dad and Amelia were the only ones who truly knew what had happened between him and Clare. "Being burned once doesn't mean that you can't be happy. It just means you need to be careful."

Camryn nodded slowly.

"Invite the girl to the gala, Cam. It won't hurt. Plus, your mom will stop hounding you." They laughed together. His father got up and left, leaving him to his thoughts.

When the next day dawned, the first thing he did was call his secretary and inform her that he was taking the day off. He had a girl to romance.

A Date at the Hospital

An incessant banging awoke Stella in a flurry of bed sheets and pillows. Her feet hit the cold floor with a groan.

The door flung open. "Stella." Eleanor pierced her with a glare that cut through her sleepy fog. "Do you know what time it is?"

She turned to the digital alarm on her nightstand. "It's 5:00 a.m." A time for sleep.

"Yes," her aunt hissed. "It's 5:00 a.m., and you're still sleeping. Are you trying to jeopardize your cousins' futures?"

At once, she remembered that her cousins were traveling to Detroit to shop for jewelry for an upcoming party. She'd forgotten to update her alarm!

"I'm sorry," she said, her mind now alert but her tongue still sluggish. She grabbed her gown and draped it on. There was no air conditioning in the attic.

Her aunt didn't move as she approached the doorway with her phone in hand. "I don't know where you went after I explicitly told you to stay at the party that night—"

"I—"

"Don't interrupt me." Her voice had a sharp tone to it. She eyed Stella's disheveled waves with distaste. Stella tucked a dark strand behind her ear. "I don't care enough to want to know. All I care about is that you take the work you do in this house seriously. There are no free rides in life. Do you understand?"

Stella nodded, ignoring the feeling that she was being scolded like a child. She resisted the urge to wring her hands together. Even if she was being treated like a child, that didn't mean she had to act like one. She straightened her shoulders. "I understand. It won't happen again."

After a pause, her aunt nodded. "Good." She stepped aside from the doorway, allowing Stella to brush past her. The tiles were cool beneath her bare feet. She could hear her cousins getting ready as she passed the second landing, the cool air pungent with too-sweet perfume.

The kitchen was quiet except for the music drifting from the TV in the living room. She found Julia there, her elegant neck tilted toward the TV as models in dreamy sky blues and pastel pinks ambled down a glowing runway.

"Good morning," Stella greeted in a small voice. She'd felt cautious around Julia ever since she'd been caught eavesdropping on her conversation with Kiana. Kiana had seemed to forget the incident as soon as it happened, but she'd seen Julia watching her in a way she never had before.

"You're late," was Julia's reply. Her long fingers wrapped around her mug as she took a sip of what looked like green tea. She kept watching her over the cup.

Stella turned toward an upper cabinet for a pan and set it on the stove with a clatter. Her hands were shaking. "I'm sorry. I forgot to set my alarm. Your mom was kind enough to wake me up," she added, though there was nothing kind about the way Eleanor had woken her up. Her behind was still aching.

Julia hummed. She could feel her watching her as she prepared their breakfast—scrambled eggs with toasted bran bread and beans. "You know, it's strange."

When Julia didn't continue, she cleared her throat and asked, "What is?" just to be polite.

"That Camryn Alvarez disappeared around the time you left. Your scooter was still parked outside when we left too. I saw the way you ran away when he looked in our direction before the show began."

Uneasiness stirred in her stomach. She tried to sound casual. "Robin fetched me. I didn't feel safe driving my scooter at night, so I called her." When she met Julia's deadpan face, she added, "You know Robin, my friend from work." It was a good alibi. Robin had fetched her the next day for work, and she'd driven her to the warehouse to get her scooter after her shift.

Julia turned back to the TV. "I know who Robin is."

Stella breathed a sigh of relief.

Half an hour later, her family filled the seats in the living room, forks clanging against their plates as they ate and watched TV. Their purses were strewn on one of the side tables. Stella knew they were going out to shop for some kind of party or gala, but they hadn't said whose it was. She leaned on the counter, chewing slowly. She already felt tired. She turned to her phone as its ringtone blared out.

Camryn's name stared up at her. She froze.

"Are you going to answer that or what?" Kiana asked without looking at her.

When Stella didn't answer immediately, they all turned to her. "Oh, yes." She took her phone and ran toward the stairs, hoping it wouldn't stop ringing. When she reached the second flight of stairs, those nearest to her bedroom, she answered it.

"Hello?" Camryn's voice rasped. Her cheeks pinked. He sounded like he'd just woken up.

She cleared her throat. "Hey."

"Did I wake you up?"

She shook her head, then realized he couldn't see her. "No. What's up?"

"What are you doing today? I have the day off from work today, and I'd love to see you."

Her heartbeat quickened. She cradled her face between her knees. "Okay," she said in a small voice. "You can come to Lakewood General Hospital at 8:00 a.m."

"See you then." The phone clicked off.

"Who were you talking to?" Stella started at Julia's voice.

Her mind raced for a name. "Uh, Robin."

"Right. Robin again," she remarked, looking at her with an unreadable expression. "Fine. We're leaving. See you later."

She turned her back before the "bye" left Stella's mouth. She should have felt scared, but all she could think about was the fact that in just a few hours, she was going to see Camryn.

Camryn parked his car and walked across the parking lot to the hospital entrance. The automatic doors slid open to allow him in, and he winced against the sharp, metallic smell of antiseptic. The receptionist turned to face him. He lowered his cap down to his eyes. This year, the paparazzi had been incessantly on his heels. He didn't want anyone to be alerted of his whereabouts—not today, when he would have the whole day to spend with Stella.

There she was! He knew it was her before she completely rounded the corner, her chestnut hair giving her away. She was wearing jeans and a simple white tee. He was relieved. He had been so anxious over what to wear that he'd called his stylist, who'd garbed him in a plain shirt and long khakis. When she saw him, she jogged lightly toward him, stopping a few inches away from him. He realized that she wasn't sure what to do. Camryn tugged him toward her and wrapped his arms around her, only for a moment. He missed her fresh, floral fragrance as soon as he let her go.

"Hi," she said. A dash of wild color had entered her cheeks.

"Hi back." A nerve quickened in his throat. He tucked his hands into the pockets of his khakis. "So, you're a party planner, you work with the most famous ride-hailing company in the country, and you save lives?" The receptionist started coughing suddenly, and he glanced at her. She was looking at them with bewilderment. Oh, no. He'd been spotted.

She laughed, the tension between them lightening for a moment. "Not quite. I only volunteer here. Have been for the past few years. This way." She beckoned with her hand toward the hallway she'd just come up.

He followed her around the corner to a hallway with a throbbing fluorescent light and up a flight of stairs. The deeper they went into the hospital, the colder it got. The smell of bleach seemed to cling to everything. Just before they walked through one of the doors in a long hallway, she turned to him and said softly, "Take your cap off. Some of the older patients have old-fashioned ideas about etiquette. Don't worry. She won't recognize you." She smiled understandingly at him. This was the first time she'd alluded to his fame. He was surprised that she'd never mentioned it before.

He took his cap off and ran a hand through his hat hair, brushing it into its usual mussed comb-over. She watched him with wide eyes, her hand hovering on the door handle.

"Okay," he said when she didn't move. "I think I'm ready." She turned quickly toward the door with—he noted with satisfaction—faintly reddened cheeks, and they walked over the threshold.

"Good morning, Alice." Her voice was cheerful but not too loud.

"Oh, Stella. You're back, dear." A slight woman, so slight that her cheekbones protruded sharply. Her dark eyes seemed like they'd sunk into her eye sockets, and she struggled to get herself into a sitting position.

Camryn darted to help her up as Stella drew the gray blackout curtains. Sunlight streamed into the room, breaking off just before it reached the adjustable bed. Her hand felt fragile and bony in his, like it could shatter into a thousand pieces at the lightest touch.

"Thank you, dear." She smiled up at him with glassy eyes. "If you'd told me you were bringing your boyfriend with you today, I would have at least tried to do something special with my hair." Her hands fluttered over the fluffy wisps of curling hair on her head. Camryn smiled. He noted with surprise the tattoos sleeving her left arm. One stood out to him—a baby with a pair of wings drawn with broad strokes, faded with age, and blurred around the edges by wrinkles.

Stella's gaze darted from him to Alice. "You and your jokes, Alice. This is Camryn." She reached for something on the stand on the other side of the bed. "And he's not my boyfriend."

His gaze snapped up to her face. She was intently studying the cover of a hardcover book in her hands, a copy of Shakespeare's Macbeth. Its spine was lined by several crinkles, and the corners of its cover frayed like an old rope. "She's right. I'm not her boyfriend... yet."

A coral flush bloomed on her cheeks when she looked up and found him watching her. Alice's cackle broke off into a fit of coughs, breaking their eye contact. Spotting a glass on the side table beside him, he grabbed it and handed it to her, wrapping his hands around her trembling hands and balancing it for her as she drank deeply. "Thank you, dear." She gasped when she finished drinking, settling back into her bed. "It's these lungs of mine, you know. They've given up on me."

"Don't say that. The doctors said..."

"The doctors say a lot of things. I know what my body is telling me." Alice's thin, square face was set.

He wondered if Stella knew how easy to read she was. Her mouth was pursed, her eyebrows lowered and pulled together, and her eyelids squinted. She blinked fast a few times and then opened the book. "Where did we leave off last time?" she asked. As if remembering he was there, she looked up at him. "You can grab one of those chairs if you like." She gestured toward the small table, and the two chairs backed up against it.

He set his cap on the stand and placed both of the chairs beside her. When she sat down, he gave her hand a reassuring squeeze. How long had she known Alice for her to be so hurt by the thought of living in a world without her? He was grateful for his father's advice now. He'd wanted to know what kind of person she was, and here she was fighting tears because she might lose one of her patients. She wasn't even paid to do this, he thought, remembering that she'd said she volunteered.

He melted back into the seat as she began to read. He wasn't fond of the tragedies—he wasn't fond of fiction at all—but he loved the sound of her voice. "To be or not to be. That is the question." Camryn bit back a smile at the horrified look Stella gave Alice as she laughed another one of her cackles.

They were in the warehouse, which Camryn had whisked her away from just a couple of nights ago. The sun was high in the sky, beaming down its intense afternoon rays. She hadn't even had to switch the lights on today.

The only thing left in the middle of the room was the stage, black and heavy against the dusty cement floors. Camryn carried the very last chair to the entrance, where the rest of the chairs and furniture were stacked. "Done," he breathed, his cheeks red with exertion.

"Thank you for today." She smiled at him. She couldn't remember the last time anyone had done something so nice for her. He'd spent his day off from work at a hospital with some-times cantankerous patients and cleaning up a large ware-house. "I really appreciate everything you've done for me."

He returned her smile. "I've had the best time today."

"Really?" She laughed. "You've enjoyed being slaved around by me all day?"

"Maybe," he replied, still watching her. She crossed her legs. He had been watching her all day. "I mean, I met some interesting characters—that was fun. What I really enjoyed, though, was watching you in your element. You have a servant's spirit. It's beautiful to watch you be who you are."

Her skin tautened as his words fell upon her ears. She was warmed by his sweet words, but would he be saying the same thing if he knew that she'd lied to him—if he knew that she was going to keep lying to him? She didn't want to know. Stella brushed her sweaty palms against her jeans as she stood, twirling slowly as she studied the warehouse. "If this had been my party, I would have gone industrial with the setup."

She continued when he quirked a dark eyebrow at her, leaning back in his seat with a faint smile. "This place already has that raw, unfinished look about it. The cement floors," she gestured at them as she spoke, "the steel walls. I would have gone with Birchwood chairs, ditched the carpet and the colored vases, and left the walls bare."

A breeze rustled his hair. "Why didn't you study interior design? You obviously have an eye for it."

She looked away from his confused gaze. "I always wanted to. It almost happened, too, completely debt-free. Then my mom died when I was twenty-three, and a few months later, my dad died. All the money we had..." She trailed off. No one ever spoke about the financial costs of death. The emotional aspect of it was enough to wind her for months, but "Grief is so much harder on an empty stomach," she murmured, brushing her hair behind her ear.

Suddenly he was right in front of her, her hand in his, looking smaller than she knew it was. Her stomach flipped nervously. "I'm sorry, Stella." He tilted her chin up. His head dipped as he wrapped his arms around her.

"It's not your fault," she mumbled into his shoulder, surprised.

When they pulled away, he said, "My company is throwing a gala in three days." Her eyes widened as his hands brushed down her arms, dancing lower and lower with her heart thundering after every touch like a caged bird. "Will you be my date?" he murmured, looking down at her with darkening eyes.

She was drowning in his gaze, more of a steel maelstrom now than the gray that had warmed her when their gazes met that night on his balcony. She wasn't warm now. She was burning, inflamed with an ardor that made her cheeks burn and settled like wine in her belly. And then, like a finished spell, his mouth was on hers. Their lips brushed gently, as soft as a butterfly's wings, breaths dancing, chests heaving despite the delicate nature of their kiss. His mouth grew insistent against hers, his arms flushing her body against his.

She pulled back then, even when he leaned forward to

close the space between them again. "I can't," she said, breathless and a little embarrassed—she had never been the type to get all swoony and lightheaded over a man, even him. Then again, she had never seen him read stories to dying patients and haul out chairs for her over and over again for four hours. A frown creased his forehead, his eyes still hooded. "I can't be your date to the gala," she elaborated.

The pressure in his arms eased. "You can't?"

She shook her head tiredly, disentangling herself from his arms. She needed to sit down. "The designer who threw this fashion show, do you remember her?"

He drew his chair closer to hers until their knees were touching. He nodded. "Flores."

"Eleanor Flores," she added softly. "She's my aunt. She has three daughters, and at least two of them like you enough to fight to death for you." Mackenna had always been interested in Camryn, but not interested enough to seek him out at parties and fashion shows like Kiana and Julia did. "If they knew that I was here with you right now, alone with you" —*kissing you*, she thought, as she pressed her hands against her warm cheeks—"they wouldn't just be hurt. They'd be angry."

He raked his hand through his hair. "Oh," he said, looking down at his hands. His nails were squared off, and his fingers were long and strong. Those were the hands that had just pressed her body against his. Piano hands, as his father always called them.

"They're the only reason I'm not living in the streets right now, Camryn." She wasn't sure why there was a pleading tone to her voice. "When my parents died," she said, taking a shuddering breath, appreciating the grounding hand he placed on her knee. "Eleanor took me in. She's given me a home, even fed me... for years. Being with you would be a slap in the face."

For a long time, he seemed to be thinking. When he looked up at her again, the steel in his gray pools took her breath away. "How much did she pay you to plan this party for her?"

Stella hadn't been expecting this question. Of course. She remembered with a start that she'd told him that she was also a party planner. When had she become such a good liar?

He misunderstood her hesitancy. "That's what I thought. I will never force you to do anything you don't want to do. Still, I'm saying this for your sake, not mine. How long do you want to indebt yourself to a person who uses you and cares so little about you that she would sacrifice your happiness for their own?"

She looked down at her hands. There was nothing she could say. She wasn't planning parties for Eleanor. She was just repaying all the good Eleanor had done for her. There are no free rides in life.

When she didn't budge, he sighed. "Stella," he said, leaning forward until his hair was brushing her forehead. "You might let yourself be used by your aunt, but I have no obligation to do that. I don't want any of your three cousins. I'm here because I want to be here..." He took her by the hand. "With you."

The Gala

Stella woke up to the buzzing of her phone. She stared up at the ceiling in confusion, wondering how she could see the stars above her when the sun was pooling over her from the window, making her skin and hair feel hot and red.

Her phone buzzed again, and she remembered that she'd spent the night at Robin's. She'd finally told her about lying to Camryn. Jupiter and Saturn glimmered down at her from the ceiling. She always marveled at how realistic this painting of the solar system was. Stella would genuinely believe that Earth had disappeared. At the same time, she was asleep, leaving her floating in space in her bed had it not been for the sizes being so off.

Robin's bed was made of two four-poster beds. Whenever Stella slept over, she separated the beds in half, giving her a separate fleece for warmth. It was her childhood bedroom, with posters of U2 and Daniel Bedingfield still stuck on the walls, along with the eccentric pieces she'd collected through the years. Twin African drums called djembes and a pair of bracelets that rattled like the tail of a rattlesnake at the slightest provocation—among many other art pieces.

Stella dug for her phone under the pillow. There were two texts from Camryn.

CAMRYN

Stella.

Don't freak out.

She immediately began to freak out. A fluttering of nerves in the pit of her stomach made her feel queasy and cut through her sleep. She watched the beat-up screen of her old phone for the three dots that would signal an incoming text. They didn't come, so she texted him back.

What happened??

She waited. The seconds seemed to stretch longer and longer. He read her text. When the three bubbles popped up, she heaved a sigh of relief loud enough to make Robin shift in her bed across the room.

Instead of a text, he sent a picture. It took forever to load, and her heart quickened as she grew increasingly frustrated. She really needed a new phone. Finally! The image loaded, taking just a moment to come into focus when she clicked on it.

A screenshot of a webpage starring a picture of her and Camryn walking out of the hospital while laughing. Her hair was swinging, and his bright eyes were focused on her. The word COSMOPOLITAN in bright blue floated ominously above the article's headline: "Could this be Camryn's new girl?"

She couldn't read anymore. Her eyes blurred, and she dropped her phone onto the bed like it had suddenly morphed into a hot potato. "Oh no. Oh no, oh no, oh no!" She jumped off the bed when her phone started ringing. It was Julia. She watched it as it buzzed loudly, not daring to touch it. What if she accidentally answered it?

"Answer your phone," Robin said, her voice muffled against her pillow. When she didn't answer it, she forced her body up. "Stella?"

"They're going to know," Stella cried despairingly, raking her hands through her tangled hair. The buzzing cut off. "I'm so done. What am I going to do, Robin?"

Robin bolted up upright. "What happened?"

"A picture of Camryn and me together. It's on *Cosmopolitan*. *Cosmopolitan*." She buried her face in her hands. "And I just ignored Julia's call." The words came out muffled.

Robin sat beside her on the bed and looked at the picture. After a lengthy silence, Robin clicked her fingers. "This isn't bad! Switch off your phone right now."

Stella peered up at her from between her fingers. "What?"

Stella slowly parked her scooter on the sidewalk. Birds she couldn't see chirped loudly. Despite everything—the picture snapped by the paparazzi, the lie she was about to tell, the dread creeping up her spine as she approached the front door —it was a beautiful morning. She frowned when she found the door unlocked, returning her keys to her purse. Locking the door was part of her nighttime routine. Did they leave the door unlocked every time she spent the night out of the house?

As soon as she opened the door, a cacophony of sounds

streamed out: wailing, shouting, the clatter of pots, and a solemn voiceover from a TV ad that she recognized as one for a funeral plan. She cringed. The wailing stopped when she shut the front door.

"Stella."

She walked to the kitchen, trying not to feel like she did more than a decade ago. When her parents caught her sneaking back into the house after she went to a party and came back well after her curfew. Eleanor was the first face she saw. Half of her blonde hair was curled to perfection. The other half was matted and tangled and clipped behind her ear. She regarded Stella with a twitching eye.

Stella steeled herself. She needed this to be convincing. "Good morning," she chirped. Her cousins were all strewn on the couch. "Sorry, I'm so late." She wasn't late. It was precisely 6:00 a.m., the time when she said she'd come back—enough time to get their breakfast done and get ready for work.

A pin-drop silence filled the room as she set her purse on the stand. She went to wash her hands in the sink.

"No one is buying your little act, you backstabber." Julia's voice was sharper than any knife she'd ever handled.

Stella turned around slowly, her sleeves rolled up her arms. "Act? What act?"

Julia rounded the counter and jammed her phone in Stella's face. "This is you," she said matter-of-factly, "with Camryn Alvarez at that little hospital of yours. Together. How long have you been with him? When were you planning on telling us that you left the party with him?" The questions were fired at her like gunshots.

Gasps filled the room. Eleanor's eye was twitching a lot more now. "When Camryn left the fashion show... you mean he left with you?"

"What?" Stella felt her face wrinkle. "Robin fetched me that night. I met Camryn..."

"So you're on a first-name basis with him now, are you?" Kiana looked like she was trying to laser her with her eyes. Mackenna was sitting beside her on the couch, looking uncomfortable, opting to stay silent.

Stella sighed, wanting it to appear as if she were getting frustrated. "I met Camryn Alvarez yesterday at the hospital. He was volunteering there. We all know that he's always trying to give back to the community." Their looks of outrage wavered. Relief flooded through her, cooling the adrenaline. She mentally shouted a million thank yous to Robin. She was always quick on her feet, and this excuse that she'd thought of in just a moment was going to spare Stella her family's fury for the rest of her life. Even Julia looked unsure of herself.

"Volunteering?" Eleanor repeated, running a hand through the unstyled half of her hair.

"Yes." She paused. "Was there anything in particular that you guys wanted for breakfast?"

Later, when she was tossing the laundry into the washing baskets so she could get it done over the weekend, Julia cornered her in her room. She stared up at her with wide eyes, holding a hoodie with an unpleasant odor against her chest like a cotton shield. "There's something fishy going on here," she began, her eyes flickering with irritation and impatience. "I can't for the life of me figure out why Camryn would want you. I just know that you're not going to tonight's gala." The warning tightened Stella's chest before Julia even explicitly said it. "Or else, I'll make sure you regret it for the rest of your miserable life."

The rest of the morning passed by without another hitch. They didn't apologize, and Stella didn't mention anything more about the picture or Camryn or Julia's threat. It kept bothering her, though, as she skipped out on volunteering at the hospital and delivered orders all through that day. When her workday finally came to an end, she drove in the opposite direction from her home toward Robin's. She couldn't stand the thought of watching her cousins don themselves in beautiful gowns and accessories while she stayed home in her jeans and blouse.

When Stella arrived at Robin's, she noticed that her car was not parked outside, so she waited for her by the sidewalk. She watched the sky swallow the sun, indigo blue chasing away mellow orange. She suppressed a shiver. Just as she glanced at her phone to check the time, Robin's silver car pulled up behind her scooter.

"Just one week now until you move out, right?" she called to Robin as she stepped out of her car, skipping past the polite greeting. Robin had been saving up to buy an apartment loan-free. It was the reason she'd been living with her parents for the past few years.

Robin gave an exasperated laugh. "Stella, we both know that you're here to avoid the gala." When Stella said nothing, Robin said, "What did Eleanor say this morning? Did she believe you?"

"Eleanor believed me. I'm not so sure about Julia. It worked, though, better than nothing." Their conversation was cut short as they walked past the kitchen and living room, greeting Robin's parents. Her dad was watching a football game, and her mom hovered over a pot that was stewing something that made her mouth water. She hadn't eaten all day. When they'd strewn themselves on Robin's bed—apparently Robin was just as tired as she was—she said, "Julia threatened me."

Robin bolted upright, turning to gape down at her. "What did that little she-devil say?"

Her nose wrinkled at the insult. "That if I went to the gala tonight, she'd make sure I would regret it for—and I'm quoting her here—'the rest of my miserable life.'" The sun in the solar system on the ceiling looked down at her. She closed her eyes. "It's okay, though. We've already decided that I'm not going—right?"

"Don't say we." Her eyes opened to look at Robin. "You made that decision. I'm not the one who was invited to the party. I'm not the one who's going to regret not going."

Stella blinked back tears. "It would never work between him and me. Especially if he found out that I lied to him. Maybe Julia should be the one to be with him." She sighed, sitting up. "We weren't officially dating or anything, but I was thinking of breaking things off with him and telling him the truth."

Robin grasped her hands in her dry, papery grasp. She was forever complaining about the biggest downside of being a surgeon: not the long hours but having to wash one's hands so often that they were perpetually dry. "You can't do that, Stella." Her grasp tightened. "I'm not going to let you. Listen, I only met you after your parents died, so I don't know the version of Stella that doesn't have to struggle through life without her family." Seeing Stella's mouth form words, she added, "Your real family. Not the people who threaten to make your life miserable if they don't let you do what's good for you.

"It's like you're always waiting for the next thing to happen in your life, Ads. Waiting until you have enough money saved to go to college, waiting until you've moved out and can live your own life. But Camryn Alvarez is right here, right now. You never asked me what I thought, but I think he might be good for you. Not because you need a man to be happy, but because if you chose him right now—someone who you want to be in your life, even if you think you're not allowed to have him—you could start becoming the kind of woman who makes active choices to build the life that she wants. I'm just saying, choosing Camryn is a choice, and not choosing him is also a choice—but which choice will make you happier?"

Stella blinked back tears, looking at her friend with surprise. "When did you start becoming such a poet?" she said in a choked voice.

"Since you're my best friend and I want you to be happy." They laughed, and Robin wrapped her arms around her.

When they pulled away, Stella said, "I don't even have a dress. All the shops will be closed by now. Even if I wanted to go, it's just too late."

Robin smiled cheekily, her eyes twinkling. "I have solutions for those problems."

Stella let her purse slip out of her hands as she giddily raced up the stairs, looking again and again at her borrowed gown. It shimmered and twinkled in her arms.

"Stella, is that you?" Kiana's voice called out from the second-floor hallway, but Stella didn't slow down. She was running late as it was. If she didn't hurry, she'd never make it on time.

Dropping the dress on her bed, she grabbed a towel and her shower things, running down to the bathroom as fast as she'd come up the stairs. She locked her room and then tucked the key to her bedroom into the pocket of her jeans, not wanting to risk any one of her family member walking into her room and seeing the dress.

"Hey!"

She whirled around just as her foot passed the threshold to the bathroom. All the breath rushed out of her lungs. She hated to say it, but Julia looked beautiful.

Her black hair glinted pure of velvety nights in an elaborate braid that snaked around her head, drawing all the attention to her angular cheekbones, the naked curve of her long neck, and her bare, gleaming shoulders. Her dress bloomed from her waist like a dark blossom, twinkling with a billion stars. "What do you think you are doing?" There was nothing delicate or lovely in the look she was giving her.

A chill raced down her back. Without thinking about her next actions, she stepped back, slammed the door shut, and twisted the knob lock with a satisfying click. There was no time for regret now. She shimmied out of her clothes as Julia banged on the door and hollered for her to open up. Instead, she jumped into the shower.

When she was finished, she craned her head out into the hallway, listening. She could have heard a pin drop in the silence that greeted her. Satisfied, she ran upstairs to her bedroom, digging her keys out of her jeans pocket with trembling hands. She laid the dress carefully on one end of the bed and opened the makeup pouch Robin had loaned her, letting its contents spill out on the sheet.

She knew very little about makeup, so she kept it simple, brushing over her eyes with a matte sky blue eye shadow that matched the dress. Then she lined her eyes with black liquid eyeliner. After that, she defined her eyebrows and glossed her mouth with a nude, shimmery lip gloss just a shade or two darker than her skin tone. She took a step back. Her reflection regarded her with hooded eyes that glowed with flecks of green against the light blue clouding her eyes, high cheekbones curving into a dazzling smile.

She laughed, remembering that Robin had insisted she look like a princess for the night. After she shimmied into the blue gown and looked into the mirror again, she knew that Robin would be proud of what she had managed to put together. No one could deny that she looked like a princess.

Camryn craned his neck as a woman in a dark gown stopped right in his line of vision, blocking his view of the entrance. He didn't know why he kept looking in that direction. He knew she wasn't going to come. She'd told him that she wasn't going to come. So why did he keep looking for her? Why had he told the men taking care of invitations to let a Stella Flores in if she sought entry?

Why couldn't he stop wishing she was here, in his arms?

He'd already danced quite a few times. The gala was the biggest party his company threw, inviting all of their investors and most of the local press in the Florida region. But it wasn't the same. None of the women he'd danced with were Stella. They didn't volunteer to work with old, cranky patients at hospitals or love baseball, or look away shyly when they were laughing at his dumb jokes. He felt closer to her in the two weeks he'd known her than he'd felt with any woman he'd known, even Clare.

A flash of blue caught his eye when the woman in the black gown was suddenly much closer than she'd been before. She looked up at him with coy eyes. "Camryn, the gala has been simply amazing."

He smiled amiably, not wanting to let on that he didn't recognize her. "I'm glad you've been enjoying it." When she extended a slim hand to him, he shook it and waited uncomfortably for her to let him go. "Alvarez Consultants wanted to have a special evening just for investors. In an hour or so, we'll begin announcing how we've spent the budget for the first half of this year."

She laughed as if he'd said something funny, her bronzed cheeks glinting in the dim lighting as she finally released his hand. He frowned at her. There was something familiar about her eyes—their cat-like tilt.

"I wanted to tell you something about Stella."

He took a step back from her. "Stella?" *Cosmopolitan* hadn't mentioned Stella's name even once in their article, so he'd thought that her identity at least had remained secret. Who was this woman? "How do you..." The shock made him trail off his words. How did she know Stella?

"Stella is my cousin." Her mouth twisted as she said the words, so her smile looked more like a grimace. He suddenly remembered who she was.

"You're Julia. From the other night."

She beamed up at him. "You remembered."

When the silence stretched longer as she continued to smile at him, he cleared his throat. "How did you know about Stella and me...?" His voice trailed off. Was Stella aware that one of her cousins knew about them?

"Oh, of course." She looked down at the phone in her hands. "I wanted to show you something. I found something in Stella's phone earlier..."

"You were looking through Stella's phone? Did you ask for her permission?"

Her cheeks glowed under her makeup. "Not exactly." Seeing his expression, she hastily added, "But I'm glad I did anyway. Stella's been lying to you."

He felt a chill sweep through his body. "What do you...?" He cleared his throat. "What do you mean?"

"I'm assuming that she told you she works with Uber Eats. Is that true?" She raised her arm to show him a text on Stella's phone. He recognized it as something she'd sent him the previous week. He'd asked her if she was interested in a lunch date, and she'd responded that she had a meeting with the local director of Uber Eats.

He nodded mutely. His mouth felt like it was filled with cotton.

"She was lying." There was a hungry look in Julia's eyes as she continued, "All she does is deliver food. She's been doing it for years, claiming that she's saving up for her future." The tone in her voice climbed to a mocking pitch. "If you want to know the truth about her, here it is: she's a leach. She's been leaching off of my mom for years, and now she's leeching off of you."

Julia and her words, the music drifting lazily from the stage, the conversations buzzing through the crowd, and the bodies brushing past his as people found their seats—it all emulsified into white noise in his ears. He swung his eyes toward the entrance, feeling like the air in his lungs wasn't enough. When he did, desire, both bitter and sweet, uncoiled like an asp in him.

Her name rushed through his mind when his eyes landed on her in a bright blue gown, her eyes almost luminescent in the dim lighting as her searching gaze fell on him. Stella. She smiled in that hesitant way of hers, and his heart ached.

He took a backward step away from her, from Julia and her cat-like eyes, from the noise that threatened to engulf him like a wave. As he turned to look for the exit, his eyes landed on a face he knew like the back of his hand. She'd left her black hair loose, and it contrasted harshly against the milk-white gown she was wearing. Clare.

What on earth was she doing here? What had she misunderstood about "I never want to see your face again"? The room was closing in around him. Without a moment's hesitation, he elbowed his way out of the crowd. He was sick and tired of liars.

A Word of Advice

THE SIZZLE OF FRYING EGGS MET HER EARS AS SHE broke the shells over the pan. Even that felt like too much work. When she walked into the hotel the previous night, she hadn't had to speak to Camryn to know that he knew. She'd seen his crestfallen expression, the vacant look in his eyes when he saw her, and the triumph in Julia's eyes; she knew immediately that she had been found out.

In some ways, she was relieved that she didn't have to lie anymore—not to Camryn, not to her family, and not to herself.

She hadn't even thought about her phone when she left for the gala. She didn't worry that she'd just left it there on the little credenza table by the front door beside her purse, where Julia could see dozens of the text messages she'd exchanged with Camryn and piece together the story that she'd spun for him.

At least her family knew now too. She'd been afraid of getting kicked out of the house, but all they'd done was give her the silent treatment. It was a silence heavy with anger. It didn't matter, though. Or at least it didn't matter right now.

She was used to picking up the pieces of her life and making do with what she had in her hands at the moment. At the moment, she still had a job. She was only a few thousand dollars away from being able to afford one semester at her local college. At the moment, she had an amazing best friend who was moving into her own home in just a few weeks—she knew that Robin would have her back in the event that her family threw her out. At the moment, she still lived the same life she did before she met Camryn Alvarez—mornings at the hospital and afternoons delivering orders. She could do this. Her hands started shaking. She had to.

She flipped the eggs in the pan, let them fry for one more minute, and then slid each one onto its plate.

"Despite everything, I'm happy," Julia said. Stella was startled when she realized that it was her that Julia was speaking to. "I may not have Camryn Alvarez, but neither does anyone else in this room."

Stella looked at her, feeling as if she were out of her body. In her peripheral vision, she saw Kiana frowning at her sister. Eleanor, however, smiled tolerably at her daughter. "Learning to find the bright side in every situation is an important life skill. I learned that at your age, Julia. I was just twenty-four when your father divorced me, and I had to stop crying and get as much money out of that situation as I could."

Now Kiana turned to frown at her mother. Julia, on the other hand, was pleased with herself, humming as she went back to filing her artificial nails. They were blue, as Stella noted with a queasy stomach, like her dress.

When she left, she didn't say goodbye. She just grabbed her purse and headed out. The cool morning air cleared her thoughts. She remembered Camryn's words and the look in his eyes when he said them—fierce and tender: "How long do you want to indebt yourself to a person who would rob you of your happiness?" And then Julia's venomous voice rang out in her mind: I may not have Camryn Alvarez, but neither does anyone else in this room.

She caught a reflection of herself as she approached the automatic doors after parking her scooter. Despite the golden sunlight flooding her body, her skin looked wan and pale, and her lips was pursed in a straight line. She flexed her arms and shoulders and shook out her hands. Alice was her first patient today. She would know if something was wrong. The last thing Stella wanted was to bother a dying woman with her silly problems.

Mindy, the receptionist, looked up at her as she walked through the doors and then quickly down at her table again. Stella frowned. "Hey, Mindy," she called as she approached her desk. She leaned over the overhang and was met by a mass of multicolored post-it notes. Lone papers were scattered all over the table, and files were bundled together by an elastic band so tight it looked like it would suddenly snap. She could never survive in such a messy place without combusting. "Is Robin in yet?"

"I saw her heading to the surgery ward about half an hour ago," Mindy replied, gesturing down the room toward the hallway that led to the surgery rooms. She was jittery, her hands constantly reaching for something—a paper clip, a pen, and a paper dated about two weeks ago.

"Are you okay?" The more Stella volunteered at the hospital, the more astute she became at reading people. She could tell Mindy was nervous.

She sighed and ran a hand down her freckled face. "No. I feel horrible." Stella was surprised when she stood, pushing back her rolling chair. "I owe you an apology." Her eyes grew pleading. "I recognized Camryn Alvarez when he was here a week ago. I totally called the paparazzi. I was low on cash and thought they would pay me. I was right about that. I just didn't expect you to get involved in this whole mess." Her whole body shuddered with a sigh. "They've been trying to bribe me to give your name away, but I promise you, I would never do that. Another one of them was here two days ago, waiting to ambush you, but I chased him away. And..."

When it looked like Mindy would go on and on, Stella laughed. "Mindy, it's okay. Seriously. We all make mistakes." She thought again of her own mistake. "Anyway, nothing official happened between us. It didn't work out in the end."

Mindy melted back into her chair, relieved. "You have no idea how horrible I've felt for the past two weeks." She laughed, and Stella joined her. "I don't blame you. Celebrity life looks way better from the outside. After seeing how the media and paparazzi and that whole lifestyle actually is, no thank you. David Beckham will just have to find another girl." They laughed again, but Stella's smile felt tight.

She told Mindy she'd see her later and headed toward Ward C, where the long-term patients stayed. She thought of her night at the baseball center with Camryn, how sweet he'd been with her patients. The hours he'd spent with her at the warehouse stacking chairs and throwing away scentless delphinium flowers. Even the tiny things. *The goodnight texts, the good morning texts, and the 'how has your day been?' texts.* She bit back a smile, her heart aching. Her brush with the paparazzi had been so minimal. While she was lying to him about who she was, had he been trying to protect her from the media without her even noticing it?

She found Alice with a book already open in her withered hands and a soft smile tugging at her mouth. She looked up at her. "You're late, Stella."

"I know, I know. I'm sorry." She dropped her purse onto the table, drawing one of the chairs to the bed. "So what are we reading this week?" Every two or so weeks, they finished one Shakespearean work and moved on to another.

"*A Midsummer Night's Dream.* I'm in the mood for

romance and comedy this week." She winked at Stella.

"To be honest," Stella began. "I would love a tragedy right now. Camryn and I didn't work out." She looked up at Alice. "You do usually prefer the tragedies. Why is that?"

Alice studied her with her ancient, beady eyes. After a moment, she shifted in her bed, and her expression became vacant. She cleared her throat before she spoke. "I never told you this, but when I was about your age, I fell in love. I never thought I would. I thought love was for the bored and boring." She rasped a laugh. "My husband was a bit of a nerd —he studied at Yale, you know—but he wasn't boring. Two years into our marriage, we still didn't have children. And a few years after that..." Dread clawed its way up Stella's spine as Alice's voice began to shake. "We had a little girl." She had always wondered about the tattoo inside Alice's arms—a baby with a pair of wings, surrounded by the blurred swirls and lopes of her other tattoos. "We were so hopeful before she was born that we went ahead and named her Angel, not even knowing whether the baby was a girl or a boy yet—just happy to have a child. She was born deformed, with only one arm and two mangled legs. She never took her first breath."

Stella imagined the hopelessness of trying and trying for kids and, after years, finally having a child and it coming out wrong. She took a shuddering breath.

"So that's why I prefer Shakespeare's tragedies." When her gray-blue eyes refocused on hers, they were not only a little sad but also very kind. "Sometimes though, I remember laughing with my husband until I was crying, or the simple joy of mending a hole in a shirt with hands that don't ache. You're still young, dear, so know this: life gives, and life takes. Don't let its taking kill you, and don't turn your nose up at it when it gives."

She thought of Camryn. She'd had him for just a moment, but now he was gone.

She withered like a dying flower in her chair.

She spent double the time she should have with Alice, so she only had time for two more patients before she had to leave. Her hands ached from her time with her last patient, a middle-aged woman who had been there for two months because of a bad liver. She'd been appalled when she learned that Stella couldn't crochet and had insisted on teaching her—even though it was the twenty-first century. Stella smiled. She'd enjoyed herself, though.

Her trainers muted her footsteps as she walked down the hall, so she heard it clearly when a pair of heels rapidly tapped the tiled floors. She turned to find the hospital manager, an older woman with graying hair and dark monolid eyes, approaching her. "I'm glad I caught you before you left, Stella. I have very good news for you."

"Dr. Umi," she greeted, smiling. "How can I help you?"

"What would you say if I told you that you could have the opportunity to study nursing at GRCC?" Her eyes crinkled in a warm smile.

Stella's mouth gaped open. She'd been saving up money to study at Naples Community College for years. However, she had always dreamed of studying interior design. After a moment, she said, "I would say that that sounds like an amazing opportunity, and I would love to get back to you," she said, finishing with a small laugh.

"Well, here's my card." She handed her a rectangular piece of paper. "You've been an unpaid asset to this hospital for a long time. When the board started brainstorming ways to help locals kickstart their medical careers, you were the first person I thought of. We'll be going public with this in about a week, so it's a good idea to have a solid answer around that time, okay?"

She nodded. Alice's words were ringing around her head. Life gives, and life takes.

Matters of the Heart

His mom had made his favorite for family game night: cheesy nachos with jalapenos. His personal trainer was probably going to murder him. Still, even if Camryn tried, he wouldn't be able to resist them. He'd loved this snack since his mom first made it when he was a teenager.

His mom kept darting glances at him. They all knew that he'd been spotted by the paparazzi with Stella, though none of them knew who she was. Now they never would. His mom was probably feeling more than a little guilty about inviting Clare over too. He popped a whole nacho in his mouth. All the nachos in the world wouldn't make him feel any better.

"How about Scrabble? I'm in the mood for Scrabble today. What do you think, Cam?" Rylan asked without quite looking at him. He was sitting with Amelia on the leather loveseat. He noted with a narrowed expression that there wasn't a single point of contact between them as Rylan reached for the green Scrabble box. Amelia took a nacho from the large bowl she was sharing with him. Strange.

"Sounds good to me." He heard his voice like it was coming from someone else's mouth. It had been barely twenty-four hours since last night's gala. Having to push his emotions aside after the bomb Julia dropped on him and struggle through the presentation of the budget report had been excruciating.

Somehow, though, today was even more challenging. Someone had leaked everything about his and Stella's relationship to *Cosmopolitan*. Now, every online magazine was releasing article after article about it. He stopped reading the articles when one magazine called Stella "Florida's fibster heartbreaker".

It was hard to imagine Stella—sweet, shy Stella—as either a fibster or a heartbreaker, and yet, she had lied to him, and his heart felt a little broken. He kept remembering her the way she'd been when they first met—stuttering, blushing, and tucking her hair behind her ear in that way that drove him crazy.

As the moments slipped past, his resolve to stay away from her slipped further and further away. He glanced at his dad, found him already looking at him, and glanced away. He wasn't ready to talk about this yet.

"I think Camryn and I are going to have our talk a little earlier tonight. You guys play on without us. We won't take long." Camryn stared at his father in surprise, ignoring the relieved sigh that his mom probably hadn't meant to be so audible.

"That's a great idea," she said.

His dad opted out of smoking his pipe today, leaving it on the side table between their seats. Outside, the floodlights lit the backyard, and a breeze waved the old oak's branches, its leaves pooling around its base.

"Did I ever tell you how I got this pipe?"

Camryn turned to his father. These days, every time he looked at him, he found, to his dismay, more pepper in his father's hair and lines crinkling outwardly from his eyes. His thoughts meandered to Stella and the sweet, sad smile she'd had when she told him about her parents. He took a shuddering breath. "I thought you just liked it because it made you look smarter."

A smile flickered at the corners of his lips. "True, to some degree." He had a faraway look in his eyes. "Your mother and I grew up in the same neighborhood. She never played outside. My friends and I even called her Geeky Gina because she only went outside to read books on her porch."

"Wow." Camryn laughed. "I can't believe I asked you for advice about women."

"I can't believe I had any to give you," his dad said as he laughed with him. "Then Geeky Gina grew up. Your mom was the hottest..."

Camryn groaned, leaning forward to the edge of the seat. "If you don't detour right now, I'm going to play Scrabble with the others." He shook his head as his father laughed. "Gross, Dad. Seriously."

"Fine. When we got older, before I started up Alvarez Consultants, we met again on the street during the Christmas holidays. I asked her out. She didn't say yes."

Camryn arched a surprised brow. "I didn't know that."

"I was as surprised as you are, son. Absolutely dumbstruck. I didn't understand why she said no. I was good-looking—even better looking than you, pretty boy."

Camryn pretended to be shocked, chuckling when his dad narrowed his laughing eyes. "If she said no, how did you end up here then?" Camryn asked curiously, gesturing to himself and the house that his parents shared.

"I dogged after her until she gave me a clear answer." Noting Camryn's shock, he raised his hands defensively. "I know, I know—I always told you to leave a girl alone if she didn't want to be with you, but Gina never said no. A no wouldn't have killed me, but she didn't even give me that.

Eventually, I just told her to come out with it." He was looking at the old pipe. "It was my smoking. I'd taken up smoking just because everyone at work did it, and the smell clung to my breath and clothes. She hated it. The science wasn't as clear then as it is now, but her dad had died, hacking his lungs out. Your mom suspected it had something to do with smoking. She was right, as always." He gave him a knowing look. His mom was always right.

"I liked her," he continued. "So I quit. She brought me this pipe on our first date. It had been her father's. I knew then that the deal may as well have been sealed. I proposed, what, two weeks later? We said our first I love you at the altar."

Camryn widened his eyes but nodded. He knew that last part—that his parents had married after knowing each other for a relatively short time. But he didn't know their first declarations of love had been at the altar. Was it even possible to fall in love in two weeks? He had known Stella for only two weeks.

When the silence continued, Camryn reached for the pipe and inspected it as he'd never done before. "I was so sure that there was a moral behind this story—some kind of lesson you wanted me to learn."

"There's always a lesson, son."

He looked up to find his father studying him, his hand resting on his chin.

"I'm not defending your girl..."

"She's not my girl." He looked down at the pipe again.

"Whoever she is, I'm not defending her. I needed to hear that your mom couldn't stand cigarettes—and why. Find out why that Stella lied to you. You don't have to welcome her back into your life, but if I know you, you're not going to move on if you never get an explanation. You've been that way since you were a child."

Camryn worried his lower lip and shook his head, but his heart was soaring, imagining and hoping there was a way he could be with her even after this. His mind was wrestling against his heart, shouting that she was a liar and couldn't be trusted. His brain had gotten him a lot further than he could have ever imagined. His career would be next to nothing without it.

But how much could his brain take in matters of the heart?

His dad was wrong. He'd walked away from something without getting an explanation. It had almost killed him, but he'd walked away from Clare after she lied to him and stole thousands of dollars from him under his nose. All without ever knowing why she did it. But Stella was different from Clare in a hundred ways. She smiled more, laughed more, and gave more. Clare, he knew, wouldn't even think of helping anyone unless it helped her. He wondered about Stella. She had lost so much. How could she still love even after everything that had happened to her? Could he walk away from all that?

When he left his father's office, he was no less indecisive than he'd been before he entered it. He felt a lot more conflicted, though, which was utterly unhelpful. He paused in the hallway when he heard laughter drifting from the backyard. He stepped into the backyard through the open sliding doors.

"Mom, can we talk for a moment?" he called. She was sitting under the pergola. Amelia and Rylan sat on the opposite end of it, laughing. Something was definitely going on between those two.

He slipped out of his shoes as her mom leaped to her feet, following him to the pool. When they were sitting beside each other with their feet dipped into the water, she spoke first. "Did you and Clare have a good conversation last night at the gala?" Her eyes were bright and animated.

"So you are the one who invited her."

Her face fell as she took in the tone of his voice. "I know you two broke things off a long time ago, but when she reached out to me with important news, I thought the gala may be the perfect time to rekindle—"

"Mom, Clare is a liar." When a frown clouded her face, he sighed, massaging the bridge of his nose. "She was stealing money from me. That's why I broke up with her. I didn't tell you because I knew you two hit it off."

Her mouth dropped, and she paled. She looked into the pool. "Oh no." The words came out like a broken whisper.

He squeezed her shoulder in a half-hug. He couldn't help but think that she was overreacting, like he'd just told her that Clare had broken up with her. "Don't worry." He pressed a kiss on her head. "In the end, I think it will all work out."

A Day in the Office

Camryn bit back a grin. The tension was so thick, he could have cut it with a butter knife. Everyone knew that a rumor was going around the office that the company would cut down on employees. A whole floor of people would have to go back home.

No one knew that the rumor had started with him.

Well, not exactly. It was a bit of a misunderstanding. He had told his finance consulting manager, a chatty guy named Mark, that the company would send a floor of employees home. Still, he'd meant that he'd be sending them back home to work, not firing them all.

Rylan, who was head of the law unit at Alvarez Consultants, winked at him from one of the seats surrounding the large mahogany table in the meeting room reserved for his meetings with the managers. Camryn had to cough to hide his laugh.

When the clock above the large projection screen struck 9:00 a.m., the murmur of voices cut off, and expectant eyes turned to him, all strained with anxiety. He wanted to quickly assuage their worries, but he couldn't help but take a moment to be proud of what was happening in the room. Every one of his managers was worried about their employees losing their jobs. This was the culture he'd been building at Alvarez Consultants for the past five years: an organization with a family spirit serving all of America and eventually the world.

He cleared his throat and spoke aloud the words he'd just been thinking. "We all know that there's a rumor milling around the entire building that Alvarez Consultants is downsizing a whole floor of employees. A rumor that some..." He gave Mark a knowing look, and he had the grace to look sheepish. "claim came directly from me. I want to clear that up today. In short, there's been a misunderstanding."

He took a breath, articulating his next words clearly. He didn't want another misunderstanding to add to panic. "Because the English department had been making several million less than the other floors over the years, we've decided that we're going to have it operate remotely. Same pay, same employees, just off-site. Training for the employees to begin operating one hundred percent online will begin next week Monday. Giselle and the other leaders of the English department have been aware of this change for almost two months now, so it's not a shock to them. I'm glad you can keep a secret better than others in the room, Genevieve," he joked, all of them laughing when Mark turned red and shrank into his seat. He winked at Mark, so he knew that he meant well.

"Two weeks from now," he continued, setting his hands on the table, "the ninth floor will begin renovation for hosting a first for Alvarez Consultants: we're going to have a new culture wing, here and in our New York, LA, and Phoenix branches.

"For now, we're focusing on African, African American, Hispanic, and English cultures." He paused with a grin to accommodate their applause. This move is going to be good for the company. "No changes will be happening on the law, history, finance, and music floors. Keep up the good work." He nodded at his PA. "Stan will tell you a little bit about the background of the culture manager we decided on. If you have any queries, my email is, as always, open."

He shared a look with Amelia that she nodded at, and he grabbed his phone and tablet, buttoning his suit jacket as he made his way out of the meeting room. The past week had been almost impossible, ensuring all the branches were ready to initiate renovation for the culture wing. In the next month, it would be fully operational. That alone had been difficult. Planning for Stella's surprise had been even more difficult.

He'd gone from texting her every day to not even answering her calls. He'd felt horrible at first, but the distance had been good for him.

He hoped he was making the right decision. He already had a good idea of what Stella would say when he spoke to her, but he needed to hear it from her.

Stella fumbled for her scooter keys, dropped them, and then dropped her purse while leaning down to get them. Her usual hair band had snapped while she was tying her hair that morning, so she'd had to open a new box of ribbons. After twisting the hairband three times to tie her hair, it became too tight and made her headache even worse. So, her hair was up in a ponytail that was going to stay up for probably another two minutes before it slipped off again. She pinched the crook of her nose, making for the hospital's entrance. What had she done have such a terrible day?

Guilt, more bitter than the black, sugarless coffee that kept Robin alert on days she had to work night shifts, raked through her. She wondered if she would ever think of Camryn without all this guilt.

"Stella!" She froze in place. Was she hallucinating now too? She shook her head and beelined for the hospital at a faster pace.

"Stella!" This time, she turned around. It was him, dreamy in a charcoal suit that warmed his eyes into iron ore. "Hey," he said when they were just inches apart, panting from his run across the parking lot.

The tears came rushing out before she could even try to swallow them down. "Camryn," she choked out, pressing her messenger bag into her stomach.

Thunder rumbled in the sky, with dark clouds flashing ominously. He looked up at the sky. She didn't care about the weather. She needed to say this now. Lightning flashed as she took his hand into her cold, trembling palms. "I'm so sorry. I understand if you could never be with someone like me," she said frantically. "I know I wouldn't deserve it if somehow you still wanted me after everything I did. So that's all I'm going to say. I'm sorry."

The little line that had formed between his eyebrows cleared as he smiled, taking her breath away. Her traitor of a ribbon chose that exact moment to slip off of her. She tried to pull her hands out to smooth her hair back, but he did it for her. "I was crazy to think I could walk away from you," he said, gently grasping her face. "Now, will you come to the car before it starts raining? This suit cost me a fortune," he joked. She laughed as he pulled her toward a black car with flashing headlights.

The car growled to a stop after they drove uptown and parked by the curb of a sleek building that she recognized after a moment as Camryn's. She smiled up at him as he helped her out of the car, tucking her hand into the crook of his arm. Heads swiveled to watch as they strode to the entrance. Stella bit her lip to hold back a smile. Here she was in her old sneakers and messy, windswept hair, beside one of the wealthiest men in America.

The smile wiped away from her face when she saw the long-legged woman tapping her foot impatiently by the entrance. Her stomach flopped when Amelia Alvarez pierced them with a glare, and then she relaxed again—only a little—when she realized the glare was aimed at Camryn, not her.

"Can't you be on time for once, Camryn?"

Camryn didn't respond to his sister. "Stella, meet my horrible, obnoxious, no-good—"

"Hey." Amelia whacked her brother's shoulder, laughing. "You're going to love me when you realize what I managed to pull together in just the twenty-four hours you gave me." She nodded at Stella, who had been wondering what Amelia had planned and what she had to do with it. "I'm Amelia. Not quite sure what you see in my idiot brother." Stella laughed, pretending not to see Camryn's affronted expression as a doorman pulled a wide glass door open for them. "But I'm very pleased to meet you."

Stella nodded back at Amelia. "Me too," she said with a smile. "And he is a bit of an idiot, but he's cute enough to suffice," she responded good-naturedly.

They walked into an elevator with mirrors all around as Amelia laughed. Camryn pressed the button with the highest number on it and leaned back on one wall of the elevator with a pout, arms crossed over. "Someone should have warned me that you guys were going to bond over making fun of me."

"Now, where's the fun in that?" Stella arched a playful brow at him, to which he replied with a crooked smile, amusement glinting in his eyes.

"You were right, Camryn. I think I'm going to like your new girl," said Amelia.

The next half hour was a whirlwind of makeup. Stella

stubbornly resisted hair curling irons and tight dresses until Amelia angrily shoved her into an elegant wrap dress with an A-line style. Camryn made himself scarce.

"How much time do we have?" Camryn asked as he peeled onto the road.

Stella's stomach was knotted with nerves, and Amelia had to turn around from the front seat and slap her hand away from her mouth as she bit her nails nervously.

"Fifteen minutes," Amelia said after checking her phone for the time. "I wish I was driving. You drive like a grandma."

Stella clung onto the headrests as the car revved forward. If this was "driving like a grandma" to Amelia, then she never wanted to be in a vehicle being driven by her.

"Will someone please tell me what's going on?" The words came out with a bite. "Because if you guys tell me that Amelia and I just played a violent version of dress up for nothing, I'm going to get angry."

She was looking expectantly at Camryn, but Amelia was the one who answered her question. "We're going to a press conference." She turned to face Stella as Camryn made a sharp left turn. "We need you to share your story."

"Whoa. That was not the agreement!" Camryn's voice was tense, and his eyes were focused on the road.

"Because I knew you would never let today happen if Stella speaking was part of the plan. But now she can make that decision for herself." Her gray eyes, unnervingly almost exactly the same as Camryn's, grew pleading. "Camryn just wanted your name cleared so people would stop thinking of you as a gold-digger bimbo." Amelia shrugged apologetically when Camryn said her name with a warning tone in his voice. "But, no offense, it's going to be a bit of overkill to have a whole press conference just for you."

The car finally rumbled to a stop outside a black-faced

building that Stella recognized as Alvarez Consultants head-quarters—she'd seen it enough times on TV during ads.

"So I, as always, came up with a brilliant idea when Camryn told me your story." Camryn snorted at his sister's words. Despite the nerves wracking through her body, Stella smiled at their constant banter. "You lied to Camryn. Everyone knows that. But what if they saw things from your point of view: a twenty-eight-year-old woman working for Uber Eats as her main source of income, randomly meeting a billionaire that she genuinely hit it off with? And think of the millions of people who went through high school but never got into college simply because they could never afford it. These are the kinds of stories that Alvarez Consultants is passionate about changing. We've always worked with orphanages and homeless people, but what about the people just getting by who will likely never improve their situations?"

Camryn turned to face her. "I hate to say it, but I kind of agree with her, Stella. You don't have to do this, but I think this could really help clear your name if you're the face of this new program."

Stella shook her head, reaching for his shoulder when his face fell. "You don't need to convince me. I'll do it. If you're really going to help people in the same situation as I am, then yes. Of course I'll do it." Anyway, she had done enough damage to Camryn's name. It was time for her to start doing some good.

A host of men in identical security uniforms ushered them into the building after leaving the car parked on the curb. They hurried through the large entrance with guest seating, looking into the street outside, where it had begun to rain thunderously, through a double doorway that more security hovered by. She took one step through the entrance and froze like a statue. Dozens—about fifty or so—of reporters sat in row after row of chairs, cameras in hand. A raised platform hosted several seats that were already partly filled and a glass podium with a single microphone.

Her legs wobbled. Camryn was at her side in a flash. "Hey." He inclined his head, so their foreheads were touching. "I'm not leaving you, okay? I'm going to be by your side every single step of the way. I promise." She nodded as he clasped her cold, trembling hands in his.

A hushed silence fell over the crowd as they made their way to the platform, and then the noise was back again, deafening, even drowning out the rumbling thunder outside. The line of security guards barring the crowd of reporters was jostled as every microphone was stabbed toward the stage and every camera was poised to take a perfect shot. Her legs felt like they'd turned to jelly as they finally stopped walking, with Stella now positioned behind the podium. Camryn set a hand on her back then, as if he felt how much she needed his support, and aligned their bodies together so she could lean against his shoulder.

Several moments passed before the silence was restored, and then she took two deep breaths that filled her body with the spicy, warm scent of Camryn's cologne. She leaned forward to speak into the microphone. Amelia had said that she should tell her story, so she did. "My name is Stella Flores." A dozen cameras flashed blinding white light as she spoke.

One Mile Further

"HEY, YOU!" AMELIA HOLLERED FROM THE DRIVER'S seat. "Hop in!"

Stella stumbled after she finished locking the door. "What's happening?" she asked after settling into the passenger seat. She'd been expecting Camryn. She'd even put on her best dress for him—a peach-colored sundress that flared out from her waist and had long chiffon poet sleeves. A pink rose that sat on the dashboard filled the car with a delicate and slightly fruity scent.

"It's a damask rose," Amelia said as Stella reached for the flower, twirling it between her fingers. Someone had carefully sliced it lengthwise, probably to remove its thorns. "Imported from Europe, it symbolizes love and beauty."

Stella looked up at her. "What's happening?" she asked again, realizing that Amelia hadn't answered her when she asked before. Her only response was an unmistakably secretive smile. Stella sighed. The press conference had been enough to teach her to always expect surprises from Amelia.

She smiled down at the rose. Maybe Camryn was surprising her. She'd seen him every day since the press conference. He'd even helped her deliver orders two days ago, driving her around town for hours. She'd finally introduced Robin to him on the second day. Her cheeks had literally ached after all the laughing and smiling she'd been doing that day and all the blushing from the long kisses he'd stolen between stop signs and red traffic lights.

She shook her head when her cheeks began to warm. "Will you at least tell me where we're going then?" she said, mostly to distract herself.

Amelia thought for a long moment and then shrugged. "We're going to my parents' house—it's just a mile or so from Camryn's."

Stella's mouth fell open. She was going to meet Camryn's parents? And nobody had warned her? She'd told Camryn that she, theoretically, loved surprises when he asked during a conversation between them as he accompanied her to her next patient at the hospital. But this wasn't the kind of surprise that she meant!

"I'm going to kill that man," she growled, her hands fluttering over the wispy, braided side bun she'd coiled her hair into. She knew she looked perfect—she had, after all, been expecting Camryn today—but it didn't make her feel any less nervous. She was going to meet his parents! The sweetheart neckline of her dress, at least, wasn't deep at all, and the dress fluttered to the space just beneath her knees.

"Why are you taking this roundabout way?" she asked as Amelia headed uptown, away from the main road that would have led them out of the city and toward Camryn's country home.

Amelia abruptly reached for the radio, ending the conversation. *Okay then*, Stella thought. She bopped her head as country music filled the car. Her mouth threatened a smile, and she bit it back. She'd wondered why Camryn hadn't switched the radio on that whole afternoon that he'd driven

THE BILLIONAIRE'S BILLBOARD PROPOSAL

around town, even during the few times that the conversation had lulled to an easy silence. She'd thought that he was so comfortable with her that he hadn't minded the silence.

She giggled, not explaining herself when Amelia gave her a questioning glance. Before she met Camryn, she'd always thought she knew him better than most people. With all the articles she'd read and the interviews she'd watched, if someone had tested her on her knowledge of him, she was sure she would have gotten an A-plus.

Now she knew that she didn't know nearly as much as she thought she did before. She hadn't known that he liked baseball and country music. She hadn't known the way the corners of his eyes crinkled when he smiled—an honest, genuine, and sincere smile—not the tight, tense smiles that he put on for TV ads and press conferences. Now that she knew him—which was at least a little more than she did in the past—she couldn't imagine not knowing him anymore. She wanted to know him for the rest of her life.

But she hadn't said anything to him yet. She'd lost him for one week, and it had almost killed her. She wouldn't push him away by moving too fast.

Her head snapped up when a luxurious pink image flashed by at the corners of her eyes. She craned her head out of her window, but the billboard was facing away from her, and they'd already passed it. Towering office buildings soon blocked her view of the billboard entirely. She looked at Amelia but settled back into her seat when she noted her relaxed posture. Maybe she'd just imagined it. She twirled the damask rose between her fingers. "It symbolizes love and beauty," Amelia had said.

She managed to convince herself she'd imagined seeing it on the billboard, but as they approached the next set of buildings, she knew she hadn't. A wide smile spread across her face. Damask roses—dozens of them—dotted on the next group of buildings. She covered her mouth as she laughed. "Camryn did this, didn't he?" she said, joy overflowing in her.

Amelia shrugged with a smile and didn't answer again, but Stella didn't mind too much this time. The very last billboard spelled out her name: *STELLA*.

She saw heads craned up to it with curious expressions and slowly shook her head, smiling. She and Amelia were the only people in Naples who knew that the billboard was for her, Camryn's Amelia. She was antsy and excited as they made the drive to Camryn's parents' home. When they drove past an ornate gate, she practically started bouncing in her seat, remembering that Amelia had said that after that, they'd need to go only a mile further to reach their destination.

When they pulled up to a dark gate, Amelia turned to her. "Are you ready?"

The question unsettled her deeply, and a flood of questions reared their heads in her mind. Why the damask roses? Why was her name on a billboard? Would Camryn make all this fuss just to introduce her to his parents? Her heart started to beat hard, almost painfully, in her chest.

Whatever was about to happen, she wasn't ready. When she didn't respond to her question, Amelia reached over and gently squeezed her shoulder.

The car purred forward slowly. A small crowd had gathered in a semicircle at the foot of the stairs leading to a large, arched front door. As the car approached them, a single figure in tan pants and a simple white dress shirt that the breeze hugged against his chest broke from the crowd. She gasped as Camryn bent to one knee, a bouquet of damask roses in one hand, while the other gingerly cradled a turquoise box that cushioned a ring that she could see winking and glimmering even from where she sat.

She stepped out of the car, stumbling toward him. Her

shaky hand hovered over her mouth. "Camryn?" His name was a broken whisper.

His answering smile sent her running at him in her heels. She registered the shocked gasps and warm laughter surrounding them as she launched herself at him, giving him only enough time to drop the roses and close the ring box.

She pulled back with her arms around his neck. The setting sun bathed his strong cheeks with golden light. As he parted his lips to ask her the question, she molded her mouth against his for a long kiss. Not stopping even when the scandalized "Oh my" and hesitant applause sounded around her. She was going to marry him—she could kiss him for as long as she pleased! "Yes!" she said when they pulled away. "Yes, I will marry you."

Camryn started laughing. "Well, let me ask the question, Stel." Her heart melted at the nickname.

"Okay," she said as she pulled away from him, smiling shyly. Amelia took the bouquet of roses from the ground as he kneeled before her, opening the turquoise box again.

"Stella Flores, will you be my wife?" His expression was suddenly pleading, as if she'd changed her mind in the millisecond it took for him to get on his knee and ask her the question that she hadn't even let herself dream he ever would until this day.

"Yes, Camryn Javion Alvarez. A thousand times, yes." She squealed as he picked her up and twirled her in the air. "A million times, yes," she said, laughing as they slowed their mad twirl.

Darkness encroached, and the stars began to wink down at her, knowing that they'd made it to the second-best day of her life, after that night on the balcony when she and Camryn had met again. Except before, the sweet day had been embittered by her lies. Tonight, looking up at her fiancé's paradoxically calm and bright eyes and the smile carving his handsome face, she loved him as an honest woman.

"I love you," he whispered, as if he'd plucked the words right out of her mind.

"I love you, Camryn." She laughed at the relief that flooded his face. She couldn't believe this man. Had he truly not known? "I've loved you since the moment I met you, even if I didn't know it at the time."

He dropped his head onto her shoulder, pulling her flush against him. Suddenly, a flurry of squeals surrounded her. Robin got to her first—she hadn't even noticed that her best friend was here—and they both bounced in each other's arms, giggling. As she opened her mouth to say something—probably congratulate her—someone took her place, wrapping her in an embrace that smelled like jasmine tea. She pulled back. Her hair was auburn—almost the same shade as Amelia's—with gray streaks that she hadn't bothered to dye. Her warm gray eyes gave her away instantly. "Mrs. Alvarez!" she gasped.

"Call me Mom," she said, her apple cheeks flushed and her eyes bright. Stella thought there was an inexplicable tightness to her smile, but she brushed the thought away.

"It's a pleasure to meet you, Mom," she said, laughing, and got pulled back into a warm embrace.

Tears sprang into Stella's eyes. How long had it been since she'd been in a mother's embrace? She couldn't believe it. Not only did she get the sweetest, most romantic man in the world, but she was going to be part of a family again—a real family. Somehow, everything worked out all right in the end.

With this holiday romance, the course of true love never did run smooth and it holds true on the ski slopes for Tamara and Roderick. One simple accident sends Roderick after the feisty snow bunny in *Bobsledding with the Billionaire*, Book 6 of the *Can't Buy a Billionaire Series*.

Enjoy your copy today!

Other Books by Rose M. Cooper

Can't Buy a Billionaire Series

Training the Billionaire

One Night with the Billionaire

The Billionaire's Bet

The Billionaire and the Biker Chick

The Billionaire's Billboard Proposal

Bobsledding with the Billionaire

Snowed In With the Billionaire

Accidentally Married to Her Billionaire Boss

Bought by the Billionaire

Bargaining with the Billionaire

Persuaded by the Billionaire

Unmasking the Billionaire

Romancing the Billionaire

About the Author

Rose M. Cooper read her first novel when she was eight years old. Since then, she has read tens of novels and twice as many short stories. She, however, did not discover her special knack for writing romance fiction until a decade later.

Now a full-time author with a specialty in contemporary romance, Cooper writes sensual yet relatable love stories designed to hook her readers at first glance. She views writing as another outlet to creativity, and thus has no intentions of setting down her pen just yet. There are many intriguing love stories to be told, and Cooper is set to tell them all.

She hails from New York and currently makes her home in Copiague, New York with her husband, her black cat and her Maine Coon cat. When she is not writing, you will most certainly find her around computers or getting her nose stuck in a book.

facebook.com/RoseMaeCooper

twitter.com/rosemaecooper

instagram.com/rosemaecooper

tiktok.com/@rosemaecooper

amazon.com/author/rosemaecooper

WANT TO BE FIRST TO KNOW?!

JOIN MY NEWSLETTER!

ROSEMAECOOPER.COM/NEWSLETTER

SUPPORT ME BY LEAVING A REVIEW!

www.ingramcontent.com/pod-product-compliance
Lightning Source LLC
Chambersburg PA
CBHW022036170626
46808CB00003B/1231